Eurudice was born on Lesbos, Greece, and brought up in Alexandria and Athens. She has published two books of poetry and has written two novellas, *Scree* and *Amphi-trite*. She holds a BA in creative writing and Fine Arts from Bard College, a degree in Archaeology, an MA in creative writing from the University of Colorado at Boulder, an MA in comparative literature and an MFA in Creative writing from Brown University where she is currently a writer-in-residence and working on her second novel.

Eurudice says of herself:

'The author lived her childhood in self-imposed isolation in her family's mansion. Her only contact with the world was literature. It thus came to pass that at the age of two she began crossing out sections in her storybooks that displeased her, rephrasing them more imaginatively. By the age of eight she had rewritten the books in her father's library, including Homer, Shakespeare and Beckett. She ran off to Hollywood — the ultimate frontier — at the age of fourteen and was shocked to discover she had to learn English, the most efficient and unemotional language in the world. Many forked tongues later, English gave birth to Eurudice's own language. The rest is all words.'

f/32

THE SECOND COMING

BY EURUDICE

Published by VIRAGO PRESS Limited 1993
20–23 Mandela Street, Camden Town, London NW1 0HQ

F/32 was originally co-published by Fiction Collective Two and Illinois State
University and appears here in revised form.

A CIP catalogue record for this book is available from the British Library.

Typeset by Falcon Typographic Art Ltd, Fife, Scotland
Printed in Great Britain by Cox & Wyman Ltd, Reading, Berkshire

Grateful acknowledgements are made for the use of the following
lyrics from: 'Englishman in NY', © Regatta Music, USA; 'Like a
Virgin', © Billy Steinberg Music and Denise Barry Music, USA;
'Runaway', © Unichappell Music and Bug Music USA; 'Black
Widow', © EMI Blackwood Music and Undercut Music, USA.

Every effort has been made to trace copyright holders in all the
copyright material in this book. The author regrets if there has
been any oversight and suggests the publisher be contacted in any
such event.

We should have been excused from lugging a body:
the burden of the self was enough.
E. M. Cioran

To Dad who created the mirror.
To Bob Steiner who showed me the periphery.
To Ravi who showed me the love.
Thanks to those whose words I have stolen.

WHY SHE LOST IT

1. FOREPLAY: PROLOGUE

Ela* has the tightest cunt in the world. Yet, in real life, every blessing is also a curse.

•

Ela's cunt is her stigma, her legacy, her shield, and her shadow.

•

Ela wonders whether her cunt is implausible, a caricature, a lush and obvious imbalance of nature. She supposes that, like a mirror image, her cunt is a trick, like throwing ashes into people's eyes: mere diversionary tactics.

•

* A pseudonym; it means 'Come'.

Ela cuts a heroic figure living with that manic cunt of hers; its restless flickering light flashes from her thighs and leads lost comers – wolves and sheep, dupes and deceivers – to its haven; like a legendary lighthouse; and like a lodestar in the firmament.

•

Her cunt gives Ela a transparency she likes. She lives in its illusory infinity. But its grip on her often becomes unbearable.

•

Before Ela has sex, a struggle takes place. Outraged by her cunt's demands, Ela asks: 'Will this ever stop? I can't keep up. Just say no!' Her cunt: '. . . ! (hi-hi?)' Ela: 'Please. I've had enough. Now cut it out!' Her cunt: '. . . ! (tsk-tsk?)' Ela: 'All this repetition drains me, aren't you ever bored?' Her cunt: '. . . ! (whoosh?)' Ela: 'SHUT UP!' Her cunt: '. . . ! (ooh-là-là?)' Then Ela shrieks. She rocks back and forth, blindly throws her cunt against any random surfaces around her and buries her hands into her thighs to block the black hole. Her cunt raises its pitch into a sharp hot ache that pierces Ela's abdomen and sucks her airtight. Ela can't breathe from the hunger. But she strains to control her cunt, oblivious to her past defeats. She wants the power to switch her cunt's awareness off and on at will. She thinks it should be her natural right.

•

Ela: What possesses my cunt? Who takes responsibility for it?

•

So Ela sits on her heated cunt, presses down on it and refuses to open her legs. The pain for pleasure mounts. Ela thrusts her cunt against the wall. She drags it over the cold tiles. She takes it into the shower. On to the toilet. To the fridge for a snack. Out for a walk. Her despair only excites it further.

•

Ela's cunt is her perfect and terrifying burden. It penetrates her life like a siren, or an alarm, turned on into eternity.

•

Finally Ela succumbs. She spends hours masturbating it to

contentment, but masturbation increases her cunt's greed out of bounds; for whereas it might be satisfied by a few hours of straight fucking, it requires weeks of continual masturbation during which each new orgasm intensifies its lust. After some days, her pleasure becomes so quick and sharp that Ela starts over every few seconds. During these vicious cycles, she postpones all her other physical needs. Her ties with the world become dangerously severed. Her orgasms and fantasies stop only when a desperate enough man-in-love manages to break into her apartment and to cut through that charmed circle of self-fucking which otherwise, Ela is convinced, would go on for ever.

•

In short, Ela's cunt is a beast. A beast that Ela is doomed to lug around with her for life, like a wandering bear-trainer chained to her wild dancing bear.

•

Masturbation reminds Ela of the snake and mongoose rivalry. They are the only equal match in the animal kingdom. Locked in a deadly embrace, their legendary battles go on for days, and it is never certain who the winner is, until the moment of death.

•

Men never understand Ela's struggle. When it takes place in their presence, they perceive it as an exotic manifestation of Ela's abundant sexuality. After the initial shock, this fervid sight turns them on. They try to help her; so they grab her cunt by the labia and try to extinguish it. Although they appear to be Ela's allies, in fact they give her cunt exactly what it wants.

•

Do all women struggle like this? Ela wonders. Do all women sail back and forth between Scylla and Charybdis for ever?

•

So Ela presents her cunt to men with abandon, as if it were St John the Baptist's silver-tongued head, laid on a platter. She gives them licence to try their luck with it and not spare it. 'Do not mistake my cunt for the kudos,' Ela warns men, hoping to tip the scales; 'enter it at your own risk.' They break into a cocky laugh. Soon after, her cunt swallows them whole.

•

No matter how hard any man-at-hand applies himself, the task of taming Ela's cunt is Sisyphean. Eventually the lovers succumb to physical exhaustion: they speechlessly gather up their dead limbs, count up the losses on both sides, perform quick last rites, retract their smoking weapons and fall fast asleep. But her cunt, the beacon, the glutton, the epicure, always stays fresh. Orgasms rejuvenate it. It immediately strikes out for new prey. In her sleep, Ela can feel it contract in waves of desire. Once again I lie wounded in my own camp, she thinks.

•

Her cunt tears Ela from the world and carries her to a continuous burst of herself, beyond moderation, obscenity or kindness.

•

Men come to Ela dressed to kill, submerged in the finery men have mastered for the serious business of soldiering. They parade to the braying of bugles and fifes; plumes wave, kilts swing, brass buckles and gold braid glint in the sunshine; flags and ramrods fly. Their cannons boom, drowning the cackle of musket fire, as they chaotically stampede across the killing field towards Ela.

•

Men come into Ela raving: 'Ah, a real cunt! It's like slipping into the tentacles of a squid, like you're swimming nude and the ocean gets condensed into this little powerful fist!' 'It smells fresh like moist earth, wet paint, cucumber, thunder!' '*Pubis Angelical*!' 'It's smart!' 'It never breaks down! It even glows in the dark!' 'You should be really proud of your cunt!'

•

What inspires these metaphors? Ela wonders. How can I be proud for something I do not control? Ela responds to men's endless linguistic exertion with equanimity: 'Sorry, I wouldn't know; it is outside my control.' But men crack up at what they perceive as her joke and assess that she, too, is good with metaphor.

•

'In the region of Ela's cunt, where the faithful perform their ablutions, there are no boundaries. A hundred thousand scents perfume the air and lotus petals rain down. Lamps are unnecessary, for it is illumined by an omnipresent light. Each labia has 99,000 veins of heat and each vein gives off 99,000 lights. Each labia has a diameter of 9,900 miles, and between the labia lie one million jewels, topped by a clitoris greater than any mountain and emitting 99,000 different idyllic colors, each in its turn variously transmogrified,' men exalt.

•

Ela is annoyed by this spirited commentary and rolls her eyes in exasperation; but her cunt sucks in its lips and lunges at the nearest flesh, always on the lookout for its next meal. As she watches it eat, Ela can't help admiring its carefree appetite.

•

Men speak of Ela's cunt with the enthusiasm of adventurers setting foot on a new continent. They assume that if they dig deep enough, they may lose their souls, but they will strike gold.

•

'Let me describe your cunt: your cunt is a rose petal in a glass of rosewater. Your cunt is a green valley at dawn. Your cunt is a dense forest with woodcutters and wolves running loose in it. Your cunt is a loud bar crowded with merchants, drunks, sailors. Your cunt is a famous brothel buzzing with wily whores, acned boys and panting fat men. Your cunt is a cathedral with a big bronze bell ringing in its belfry. Your cunt is the walled compound of a Forbidden City where devout euphoric mandarins toil and conspire. Your cunt is a great nation's fleet with submarines and warships; anchors are pulled up, waves splash on deck, a cabin-boy jumps from the mast into the sea, the captain lights his pipe, the maidenhead at the prow laughs, a game of dice is heating up. Your cunt is a transparent lake, and at its bottom lies a white sunken capital; a colossal octopus rises out of the city palace and glides down the brightly lit avenues mangling under its sucking tentacles thousands of fresh flowers which were used that very afternoon for the funeral of the emperor. Your cunt is a humming-bird that sings in my ear cuntinuously.'

•

Ela sticks her finger up inside her mysterious cunt, trying to comprehend what it is that men try so hard to describe. But she feels nothing abnormal. She holds a mirror up in front of her open legs and attempts to see what everyone else sees. It only reflects a pink slit that shimmers in the light. No heliograph; no labarum; no funeral pyre; no Magna Carta; no deep freeze.

•

Men believe that by means of microscopic observation and astro-nomical projection, Ela's cunt spreads out to infinite horizons and becomes the foundation for an entire theory of the universe, an agent whereby they may perceive the Truth. Her cunt provides a short cut for escaping from the trammels of their mundane daily lives and for entering the uncharted Divine.

•

Ela enjoys letting strangers stare into her cunt. She appreciates the purity of her cunt, which is the only part of herself whose appearance she cannot manipulate. She can never see what they see. It is the price she has to pay for female evolution. Still, Ela badly wants to have a good look at her cunt one day.

HER EX-LOVERS RECOUNT WHAT THEY CAN SEE IN ELA'S CUNT:

A: 'I see a resplendent butterfly, with soft wings opening and closing in a position of rest; and tiny harpstrings of nectar.'
B: 'The clit is the head of a priestess, the labia are her flowing robes. I see the wrinkles of the cloth and everything.'

C: 'I see a woman peeking out through the curtains. She comes out of the dark and shows herself to me. Her body language is that of showing. It is the most natural and perfect image. The manifestation of something very strong, deep within. The woman changes in light and shade. She is capable of metamorphosis.'

•

No woman can call herself free who does not own and control her body, feminists believe. How does that apply to me? Ela wonders.

•

Men brag, bark, bugle, bulge, brandish their brash tools, bang on her door, and beg to be inside Ela. They vow to conquer her cunt or die at its altar. Their divining rods, their radars, sceptres and wands point at Ela. So they spin around her like moths to a candle and exclaim: 'Your cunt is out of this world!' Ela wonders: Where is it then? In an 'Other' world? What do men mean?

2. LOVE: DIALOGUE

Every few months Ela flies to a different city or country to get away from men who stick anything into her tight cunt in their struggle to stuff it up: lit cigarettes, candles, dentures, watches, credit cards, phone receivers, coins (to make a wish), crosses, wedding or high-school rings, worrybeads, pens, keys, glasses, batteries, photos of their mothers and sweethearts, pacifiers, baby or beer bottles, sashimi, caviare, steak tartar, garlic (to ward off evil spirits), oysters (with cocktail sauce and lemon), live snakes, snails, Steve's ice-cream, silverware, umbrellas, light bulbs, tulip bulbs, torches, hammers, mufflers, plugs, cattle-prods, war medals, knives, guns, Molotov bombs.

•

Ela disassociates from the world during sex and is not aware of what men insert into her cunt. Later, her sense of propriety and privacy is shocked by the imagination men use when they fuck her. Ela's paradox: Despite the constant invasions, her cunt stays the world's tightest; yet nothing and no one is too big for her cunt.

●

Ela's cunt is blind as a bat: if it were up to it, Ela would fuck indiscriminately. But Ela tries to follow some standards. The statistics are surprising: Ela has fucked *c.* 500 men (a very low sum, considering how many men daily hurl themselves at her cunt).

●

Ela's cunt brings together men's minds and bodies, and it unites otherwise unrelated men in the populist hunt for its possession. Ela's cunt is a universal common goal and a communal meeting ground. It builds its own nation. It is the Great Encapsulator. It is the Prime Minister of the New World Order.

●

Because of her cunt, Ela lives like a nomad, for there is always the danger that, given enough time, any city will transform into an immense bed for Ela, that every applicable male will share. 'The world is your bed and your temple,' men lovingly orate.

●

Ela resents being loved. The world uses love to claim me, to name me, to run my life, she thinks. This generic male love should be tabooed and outlawed. Love is a male inheritance, like Adam's missing rib, or Plato's half-seashell, Ela thinks.

●

Men whisper respectfully when they see her, like wide-eyed monks entering the sanctuary before the holy icon: 'God is wearing black tights tonight'; 'God is in the room coming'; 'God is known for the supple cruelty of her Grecian profile, her reptilian tongue, her gold impetuous eyes that teach dedication to a lie.' The fact that Ela is known never to have given her love to any man inspires in men an ecclesiastic sort of unrequitable love.

●

Ela believes that religion is blasphemy. The Divine exists in flux, creating and destroying, far beyond description and comprehension. Religion fights to nail God down, just as love like a python struggles to constrict Ela for easy consumption by undiscerning mortals. She thinks God should renounce all Faith.

•

In Ela's striking face men see, unexorcised, their fear of life. Ela's face is too refulgent to be designated a mere object of flesh, and men do not know what name to give it. They can only think that something which has for a long time lurked deceptively within them has finally revealed itself, and begun to stir.

•

Hand-made puppets of Ela are often left on her doorstep wrapped in bloodstained newspaper or old lace. The dolls have long silver hair, enormous kohl-lined eyes, hard breasts bursting out of deep décolletages, and smirks on their pink lips. A tiny cross, a needle, or a penknife is nailed into their left tits. As soon as she gets one, Ela gives it away to children to play with.

•

In the twinkling of an eye, what men imagined to be safe collapses in ruins. A woman's beauty, they remind themselves, is but a fleeting apparition of flesh soon to be destroyed. But try as they may to ward it off, the ineffable magnetism which overpowers them at the instant they lay eyes on Ela, presses on their hearts with the force of something that has come from an infinite distance to destroy them. They become immersed in their panic, as in a swift drug that transmutes their spirit. They look around them and everywhere they see their identity, the very time they inhabit, being crushed by that magnificent cunt.

LAW OF SUPPLY AND DEMAND:

The more men love Ela, the less Ela loves men. The speed with which men project themselves on Ela is a sign of how little attention they deserve. The longer they resist her, the more energy she lavishes on them: it is her social barometer.

•

Men search obsessively into Ela's eyes; for it is the goal of love to find what each of them needs in someone else's eyes; to open up before them and to burn in them. Ela's eyes are provocative, absorbent, and forgetful. So they naturally induce the inexpiable desire for the never-ending finality of love.

•

Ela thinks love is a form of gangrene that settles in silently; it moves fast like a bacillus loose in the blood and takes over one's entire body, causing excruciating agony or insanity. Soon after the pain stops, death comes. Ela is very familiar with the unmistakable putrid smell that signals the presence of love.

•

Men squint, lean back, frame, measure, draw and photograph Ela, but they cannot penetrate her surface. There is a distance between their eyes and their visual images of her. If they reach out to touch her, she is farther than they calculated. They never know if she sees them. When she looks at them, she reflects them back looking at her; so they watch themselves looking into her face, unable to read it. It faithfully imitates their own expressions and, by doing that, ennobles and magnifies them. But when they look long enough, her face opens up and they see a blank space like black leader on a movie screen: a gap.

•

'Ela is a reflection in an immaculate mirror. If her original exists, it is invisible to the naked eye,' men theorise. 'There is genius in the plotting of her flesh,' men confirm; 'she is new substance.' 'Ela's face is part of the sky, a cloud,' men compose; 'one always remembers it, like the image of a sea or fire or of the mirror.' 'She is enveloped in an invisible cocoon.' 'In Ela's face shines the ancient light of the mood in which man comes face to face with God; she is the heir of past saints, the prophet of a new order of development,' men extol. By turning Ela into an increasingly impossible being, men feel a reassuring safety.

•

I should have been excused from lugging a self: the burden of the body was enough, Ela thinks.

•

Ela's body, enfolded in thin, translucent skin, has been arranged for comfort like a space-saving amenity designed and built to the highest technological specifications. Her small, strong, frail-looking frame hints of hollow passageways, underground crypts, secret silos. It is an ingenious hiding place.

•

Men treat Ela like a two-way mirror. In front of Ela they feel self-conscious, foolish. Away from Ela they feel abandoned and in danger. They mumble, petrified, 'Please, Ela, make me a man.'

•

Ela read recently that 66 per cent of men believe in love at first sight; 67 per cent feel that files are being kept on them for unknown reasons.

MEN DESCRIBE ELA'S BODY, OR ANY JOE IS A POET:

JOE 1: 'She looks so complete that I cannot mentally undress her. She shines so blindingly that I cannot describe her after she's gone. But I know her cunt smells of holy smoke.'
JOE 2: 'Her body is made of cunts. My cock goes straight in anywhere – her neck, her knee, her foot, her belly, her ear.'

•

All the time, Ela senses the piercing gaze of men-in-love on her back. It is a commonplace love, she tells herself. These men's love has nothing to do with me. It is an one-sided affair, in which my own feelings have no part. I am not responsible for it.

•

When Ela speaks, in her tone of impeccable breeding, words become immaterial; men listen to the music, the roar and hum coming from inside her body. They suspect that an intricate memory bank hidden in her body spews out words whenever she needs language. Ela usually produces irrelevant speech that is introduced with: 'Don't tell anybody, because this is a secret, OK?' This makes men feel unique. Honoured that Ela addresses them, men break into enlightened smiles at the sound of her infectious voice, and deliver themselves to her as her faithful prisoners. 'A lifelong shadow lifts from my heart: the vague search is over. In you I can find eternal shelter. I am yours, Ela, rape me,' men exclaim. Ela wonders: Why doesn't anyone rebel? Why don't these men kill me? Doesn't it occur to them that I am fallible?

•

Ela suspects that by being in love, men feel alive. They feel free from the confines of their identities. What crushes them also enchants them: the loss rather than the possession, the confusion instead of the certainty. Love is inevitably drawn to indefinable objects. That is why Ela makes a prime target.

•

Ela has only contempt for men who lose their wits over her. How can she respect people who don't have the pride and decency to hide their insides? She doesn't know what to do with their love. Should she bathe in their hot innards to preserve her beauty? Love is too intangible to arouse Ela. So she drags men's flared hearts carelessly behind her. 'Man is alone until the moment he looks his death in the face,' Ela warns men. 'If you saw your eyes,' men interrupt, 'you'd understand.'

•

Ela thinks she also possesses the world's tightest heart; there may be a proportional relation between a woman's cunt and heart.

•

'Love is our ally,' men tell Ela, 'love is our mother, our child. My love for you is a huge sun.' Ela hears: love burns men in the fires of the sun; love is a nuclear reactor, a typhoon, an earthquake; every natural disaster, contained in a single mortal heart.

ELA'S HASTY NOTES FROM THE BATTLEFIELD OF LOVE:

Whether I give myself to men or not, they will suffer. Love always backfires. The masses have maldigested the Christian method: man can achieve anything, they believe, through love; the spirit of love will prevail victoriously if only man has the faith to persist. They think that their smothering love is omniscient. They assume that, because they love me, they have every right over me, that love is a gift which they can impose on me and come to sow its seed; like a real estate investment. They love as easily they shit: usually once a day. They also forget that:

1 Their love has no intrinsic value. Their love for me is not a diversion or an entertainment. It is a vulgarity.
2 Loving back is not an obligation or a civility.
3 Their love is a defence against themselves. They can live without it, yet they treat it like bread and water.
4 Their love has nothing in common with flight or freedom.

•

Compassion, another Christian motto, is incomprehensible to Ela. She cannot distinguish destruction from salvation, for herself or for anyone else. She cannot understand herself or others. So she tries to minimise her effect on humanity by passing on to men the responsibility of all the definitions. Men love it.

•

'I am surrounded by your unconditional love. You give me all that you possess,' men assure Ela. 'I possess nothing,' Ela protests. 'You are perfect, but I am part of you,' they insist.

•

Ela is disconcerted by any conjunction of herself with others. She cannot imagine merging or identifying with men. Recognising another's face shocks her. Familiarity disturbs Ela. She disdains the farces of good fellowship: pictures in wallets, ready-to-wear clothes, address books, car pools, pop charts, parades, shrinks, gyms. For Ela, any temptation to love involves a betrayal of the mirror. Love blinds people to their own blemishes, and to the inadequacy of the world. It chains people to their fantasies of others. It breeds sacrifice, stagnation, suffering, humiliation.

•

But being loved is Ela's character: no matter how many people love her, she relentlessly inspires more. She spends half of her life avoiding those who love her, and the other half making them love her. She redefines the art of loving without knowing it, like a somnabulist who composes poetic masterpieces in her sleep.

•

Ela wonders: Does the ocean love the men it drowns? Does it love their implacable purity, their soft, malleable bodies, their pale fibrous lips, their sepulchral torsos, their fast-rotting cocks?

3. SEX: LOGOS *(IN THE BEGINNING THERE WAS THE WORD)*

Sexually overwhelmed by Ela, men both justify and prolong their enslavement to her by falling in love. Nothing distracts them from their idea of Ela that claims their ease of mind and traps them in a timeless handjob. Men exorcise their corporeal pleasure by falling in love. Otherwise, they feel guilty; insensitive; diminished; exposed. They need promises of possessive tomorrows.

•

Men invented love to use it as an aphrodisiac. When they love, the stakes are high; they serve an urgent noble cause when they fuck, so their senses and their performances become heightened.

•

Love makes miserable lovers seem sublime: lovers persuade themselves that their beloved is better than anyone who came before or who could come tomorrow; they overlook the shortcomings of the beloved to protect their love-investment. That delusion, a censorship of the future, is impossible for Ela. Faith kills sex.

•

Ela notices: I fuck well when I am a myth, a dream, a symbol. Then I soar through open space. When my flesh is on the verge of crumbling away, I reach the very boundary of oblivion.

•

Her familiarity with sex explains why Ela has no fear of death. For Ela, death is coming, and vice versa. She notices: When I fuck, I am the void. The first penetration brings my death; I can't see, hear, think: I am all cunt. I make a show of my orgasmic death. I die and come back from the dead to die again. I love dying. *If I could come incessantly, I would be God.*

•

Ela's spiritual core lies in her cunt. Her cunt is her soul. She comes with her soul.

•

For Ela, sex is the time when everything has ended. She is never as free, as alive and real, as when she comes. Sex is Ela's bath. What life takes from her the rest of the time in every way, she takes back during sex. Immune and impartial, distant from any violent wakefulness, she senses for once the world's reality.

•

That is why Ela makes a point of coming in every public area she frequents – grocery stores, boutiques, restaurants, parks, banks, libraries, classrooms, offices, subways. The memory of herself coming enables her to survive the morbid charades of daily life.

•

Public locations can also inspire the fortuitous combination of lover, surprise, danger and sacrilege that brings out Ela's best orgasms. For Ela rates her orgasms by the cosmic sense they can give her that she is God and she is boundless; and not by their length or intensity. She does not value thirty consecutive spasms or three-minute explosions, but rather those few times when man, place, time and mind coincide to create an invincible new world.

•

Besides, how can one know anything is real without outside witnesses?

•

Around the world, men who have had sex with Ela become organised into exclusive societies. They meet to share sex secrets and exchange Ela anecdotes. They award by majority vote each newcomer's performance with Ela. Their status is marked by a silk thread they each wear as a cock-band. Red threads indicate superhuman lovers. Pinks mark tender, adjustable lovers. Orange is for oral experts. New hues are added every day. All members celebrate the anniversaries of their sexual unions with Ela. The most active members develop plans to harness Ela's sexual energy: they hope to use the turbo-charged motor of her cunt for a huge power station of natural cunt energy that will provide electricity for homes and factories. Their club anthem reveals the mental regressions Ela causes to her lovers: (sung to the tune of *'She'll Be Coming Round the Mountain When She Comes . . .'*)

> *'If love is cheese, I'm melted mozzarella,*
> *just a spoonful of Ela makes my heart go acappella,*
> *ta-ra-ram-pam-pam, ma dona bella,*
> *for she's a jolly good fella, my Elaaa . . . oh yeah!'*

'Men run to me to have their illusions shattered,' Ela tells men. Ela discourages any prolonged male presence in her world. She does not go out with men. Sex is the only way in which Ela can communicate with men. She thinks that's natural.

•

Mixing their semen with that of previous and future lovers in one highly idealised cunt is aphrodisiacal for men. Ela's cunt is a homosocial, mildly homosexual bond, a conduit that joins all men who come into it but also measures them up against one another. A natural selector.

●

The stories of men chasing Ela through thick and thin make other men chase her also. If she agrees, she replies: 'OK, let's have sex. If we fuck, I will forget you.' This frightens men. They blubber: 'But you don't understand me.' Ela: 'We fuck or not. Choose.' As men rise to the task, eager to write history with their cocks, they feel like pilgrims and crusaders setting out on a rocky course towards the great miracle awaiting them at the end.

●

Simultaneously, thousands of thoughts cross men's minds: Will I survive? Succeed? What if I lose my erection when I am so near the goal? I'd better use my *Kama Sutra* reading. I can surprise her by performing all 369 positions with acrobatic agility and without a safety net, progressing from the Chinese wheel to the Indian reversed aeroplane to the elephant-on-bird posture and back.

●

Ela orders them: 'Spread your body.' She puts silver or pink lipstick on her cunt. 'Get ready, go!' she calls. She urges: 'Do one for the mirror!' Soon she comes with a war cry.

●

Sometimes she directs them to undress, grab the bed posts or hug their knees, and be still. She admires their curves, moans and lifts the hissing whip. She enjoys their determination to stifle their cries, the timidly offered buttocks that turn red, and her own exhaustion. She comes even before the first strike. Ela sees flagellation as an overcoming of boundaries, outside the realm of common sensations, free and exhilarating. Scars highlight the beauty of flesh, for all things obtain value against a background of death. When men complain: 'I am at the end of my emotional rope,' Ela takes it as a request for S & M. She gets out her handcuffs, thread and needle, pincers, nippers, pliers, ski equipment, gladiator costume, and replies: 'I've never been suicidal; I suffer from the opposite syndrome.' She whips her lovers with their belts. She prefers belts that have large metal buckles, such as the VW logo. When they relax, men enjoy it as the first sign of her love. She never whips the same man twice.

•

Meanwhile, men are always busy thinking ahead: The detail is what matters, just like in the movies . . . the long masculine curve of my thigh in the chiaroscuro . . . I'll take her on a grand tour of the furniture: to the armchair, the sink (preferably full of dishes), washing machine (best if it's working), fridge, the broom closet (like a jail for juvenile delinquents), the balcony. Then what?

•

Am I the opposite sex? Ela asks, in mid-rhythm. Or am I the sex?

•

I am not doing enough, men think in terror; I should now do a rain dance, 30 knee-bends and 30 push-ups while inside her, flailing my muscled arms hither and thither, then run out and bring back the guy from the upstairs apartment and perform a Bermuda triangle (both men on her), then Ben Hur (one rider, two chariots), then end with a vicious cycle (one behind the other).

•

After sex, Ela sleeps while men narrate to her their unassorted childhoods till dawn. They peer into her post-orgasmic face that glows with heavenly peace and suddenly know that they can never be One with her. This thought torments them, and they interrupt their monotonous stories ('when I was nine, my Dad got drunk, pulled down my pants and chuckled'); their voices crack, their blistered cocks fade and they shout: 'How frightfully fulfilling love is!'

•

Ela thinks: I envy the stylites (Christian ascetics living on pillars). I would love to live alone on a vibrating pillar.

Then suddenly men notice that simply looking at the sleeping Ela is enough to conjure up their favorite melody (*Nanna's Lied, Und was bekam des Soldaten Weib?, Tango habanera, La donna e mobilé, Cielo e mar!*), and now that they so enjoy the music, they don't lift their eyes from her again. When the intensity of the music forces them to shut their eyes, men hear from within them a rising murmur: words spill forth from them again, as if sprung from the very air. They still want her to know everything about them; they need to empty themselves out into her. It is as if their instinct for survival leads them to vivisect themselves, to wrench from themselves their innermost core and drop it at her feet.

•

Men feel equal and intimate with her when they speak. Their own prattle reassures men. Their sexual performance alone leaves men threatened. They prefer the warmth of language.

•

Ela resents men for using sex as an excuse for confession.

•

Ela often blindfolds herself during her everyday fucks to avoid the sight of men self-consciously stroking and poking her with gummy reverence. 'This is the Test,' men think, 'the big time, I can't fuck up, my honour is on the line: suppose I make a mistake, suppose I fuck like an actor or a secretary?' So Ela ties her panties over her mocking eyes and exposes instead the pure eye of her cunt, which loosens men up. When they don't feel watched, men perform better. Besides, Ela prefers not to see what she desires. She dislikes the visions of human panic that surface during sex.

•

Every man who finds himself inside Ela wonders: How is she rating me? Men fuck in the terror that another man has surpassed them; they fuck as if they were being judged by God.

•

For Ela, a blind fuck is as courageous as any other gamble.

A one-nighter provides an intensity created by the mystery of the stranger and the ensuing suspense that transcends the two individuals and that is impossible to sustain for long. Any lasting relationship contains the seeds of its own pedestrianism. A flying fuck cannot be dominated. Anonymous sex is weightless.

•

'My life up to now was spent with caution, and what happiness have I gained?' men confide in Ela. 'Why should I plan? Why should I work? Things come and go without my planning, in spite of my plans. So I come, into you, Ela, wherever you take me,' men avow. Ela mistakes the tears on their faces for sweat.

•

Ela wishes she were a hermaphrodite. Her inquiries into sex-change remain disappointing: science cannot add on to her pelvis a functional cock that could penetrate her own cunt in solitude.

•

Men feel grateful to be allowed into Ela. They think: a cock is insensitive and crude. I must try not to become a hammerhead. Ela thinks: men are vulnerable inside a cunt, and at its mercy. They plunge into something they have never seen. So both sides relish what they imagine to be the weakness of the other.

•

For that moment when they enter Ela, men feel in control, for it is their erection which excites her. That glory evaporates as they get busy deciding what tempo to follow, which parts of her body are most sensitive, how to use their muscles, weight, skin and memory to satisfy her, how to time their orgasm to coincide with hers. They blank out their pleasure to concentrate on hers. They turn into hard-working greasers slogging in the mines.

•

Ela plunges into sex head-on like a gleeful dolphin. She doubles up into loops, rises into a pyramid, unravels like a flowing ribbon, contorts into yogi formations. She grunts, gurgles, gulps, giggles, twitters, squeals, shrieks, sobs, laughs, whistles, mews, clucks, crows, claps, chants and wheezes until she is hoarse. She twitches, quivers, kicks, nods, ruffles, rises and thumps on to the ground like a dying queen. She sings tremulous Egyptianite pitches like a muezzin's call, and produces endless operatic combinations of vowels, foreign euphoric sounds that compose an indecipherable discourse of hedonism. It is rumoured that she speaks in phrases from a forgotten holy tongue.

ELA'S EX-LOVERS' OBSERVATIONS ON ELA'S WAIL:

A: 'Ela's orgasms are a symphony titled "Death of a Tragedienne". Her wail makes every metaphor literal: it reveals the unknowable in the familiar, the impossible in the possible, death in life.'
B: 'Ela's wail is the missing link. It is a catharsis, the Ideal Happiness.' Unaffected by the world. I no longer feel nauseated by all the people who want her, or afraid that they may take her away, because I now know that she can never be possessed.'
C: 'She doesn't come, she prays. Better than those choruses of Buddhist monks and Bulgarian priests . . . People who say she mistreats men have not heard her wail: it is the greatest gift a man could hope to receive in life. It is anything but funny.'
D: 'No institution, no knowledge, no family, no cultural heritage could prepare me for this. It is the impenetrability of nirvana.'

•

Ela's response: All I did was come.

MEMORIES OF A VOYAGE THROUGH ELA'S BODY DURING HER WAIL:

A: 'For the first time in my life I was the Other. I lost my cock. It felt complete, effortless. There was no decapitation, no slicing off, just sliding into a dissolve. I was fused into her. Her cunt, superimposed on my groin, was my cunt, allowing me to physically be her. I was amazed how natural and fulfilling it was to be a woman. I felt so close to her then.'

B: 'Inside her I see large boulders, through which move strange red vehicles that could be bedouins on camels under a small blue sky. Atomic particles and metallic structures circle here and there. Pink searchlights and white light beams fly around. It is a biological spaceship. It is the soul performing for humans.'

C: 'A circular door of light slides open, and I step into a busy chamber: an astral pinball machine with shaking walls. Over my head I see a glass-domed atrium: the outer layer of Ela's stomach. I proceed deeper into this silver warehouse; I want to locate the wail. The pinball alley shoots up firecrackers of energy around me that fall into a gutter. The gutter is made of slimy organic tissue and drifting pieces of sediment. It has the beauty of a swamp; it destroys every cliché of beauty. I stand amidst the most incredible lubrication of everything I see by a continuous torrent of bodily fluids. The texture of the walls is living; it is akin to the grey matter of the brain, with blistery wrinkles, unlike the hard shapes of familiar creation. The timeless unity of this bacterial fungal formation overwhelms me. I feel my eyes have been opened physically and I witness true beauty at last. The prevalent colour is raw pink. I notice on my side a throbbing red bicycle seat that may be her liver. I look up and realise I am under her heart: her breast curves upward like the dome of a church, and through it I can see a bubble-city. It's where I want to be. I move up through a corridor of rings like inside a dinosaur skeleton. A stifling presence gathers around me. It's pitch black. I walk sideways through two huge floatable gas balloons that press on my body. I feel like a trespasser. I can't see to turn back. I shouldn't be here, I think. There is no oxygen . . . !'

•

Am I causing all this ecstasy? men wonder. They think it is her love that gives to their embraces this potency and a meaning they never dreamed of before, so they hug her madly and believe: 'She loves me so much she can die; I am more than a transient cock.' Transported by her rapture into the highest echelons of manhood, secure in their sexual genius, feeling as finalists of the world championship for the best lover, men now want Ela to focus her eyes and acknowledge them; to tell them that she loves them.

•

Ela thinks: Being owned and being fucked are opposites. Possession is erotic only for that second when I hold a man tightly in me; the annihilation of the self is not itself erotic. An orgasm is the outcome of a vague, deadly danger that forces me to reach beyond my capacities. It is a crime against the mind.

•

'Don't you see,' men ask, pounding themselves into Ela, 'don't you know me?' 'I am your slave, I am here!' they pant. 'I am your prehistoric lover, I am back!' 'Say yes!' 'Am I making you happy?' 'Do you like it?' 'Do you love me? Say it!'

•

In fact, Ela responds to the sensations in her body, and not to what causes them. In this way, she is both erotic and chaste.

•

Ela slaps, caresses, tickles, hugs, relishes, sucks and excites herself, gasps in an impetuous rage of joy, drowns in a solitary singing madness that confounds her lovers. She rolls off the bed or the bench or the ledge and, holding them tightly inside her, drags them along on the ground, leaving behind her a phosphorecent trail of cum, like an extraterrestrial crawling slug.

•

Her lovers puff, gush, fret, thrash, reel, grope, climb and heave as if struggling with the ocean after jumping ship; they shove their flustered cocks into her last niche, agonise to hold on to the rudder and steer, to bear the brunt of her lust, break her trance, force open her heart and shackle it. They clutch their eyes to escape from the sights of her flame that bring them to the verge of coming;

lights flash in their brain, they turn black in the face, blinded by sweat, but refuse to go down. They knead, rotate, swing, ride, plough, smother, sling and manipulate her like a rodeo horse or a Chinese gymnast. Their breaths whistle through clenched teeth, their tongues bloat with pounding blood, their cocks sail on lost to them for ever, but they cling to Ela even more tightly, and can still blubber: 'I am planted in you,' 'I am a sword piercing you,' or again, 'Call me: My love!' They storm the fortress of her cunt for days, pound the breath out of her, beat ugly grunts from her throat, press for what now they live for: to reach her very centre, her inaccessible soul; to hear Ela bleat: 'This has never happened to me before!'

•

Ela's orgasm* is a visit to the Other world. It is an endless piercing fall into empty space. The floor falls down from under her. Her innards push to jump out. But a tremendous centrifugal force keeps her body pinned to the spinning drum of the world.

•

While she comes, Ela chokes, convulses and faints. Some rookies become perturbed: they stop short, cover her with blankets, dab her with water, weep and call the police. Then she comes to.

•

Sooner or later the men smell the pungent stench of a duel taking place, the foul odour of their own burning nerves: they are being devoured by her, and they become enraged. They envision every man whose marks have been effaced from the walls of her cunt, every fanatic who played deadly games with his cock in flames. It dawns on them that no man has ever broken into her: she is voluptuous death. So they feel exuberant, like men who face a doomed struggle. They blurt out: 'This will kill me. Do you want a corpse in you?'

•

* *Ela's clitoral orgasm is a whole new book.*

But loss pleases Ela. She loses or abandons anything she owns. It gives her freedom. Good sex is sex she cannot control.

•

The men refuse to give up. This is their time in the lights, their chance on stage, when they must break her into recognition. They fuck against hope. They implore God to send them more cocks, one in her mouth, one in her ass, two in her ears; teams of fresh cocks to replace the tired players. For they know that her cunt could open under them at any moment and hell would show through.

•

Sex is apocalyptic. An orgasm is a shocked, stunned recognition: 'God exists!' Each orgasm is a divine unmasking, Ela believes.

•

All these hours Ela rises and falls and laughs with awe at the pandemonium of her flesh, the whipping maelstrom in her cunt. She gives men everything but the words they need. She wails, comes, faints, comes to, comes and faints again, until she loses consciousness for so long that she could be declared legally dead, and she no longer feels even through her cunt.

•

Men are suddenly shocked to feel their own pleasure: it comes over them as a quick, sharp joy that is out and gone. Then they have come to the edge of the cliff. They lie spent. Some jump off. Some calculate how far they must go for it to happen again. Some want to talk about it. Some ask to be held. Some shout: 'I came like a woman!' Ela believes men suffer from vagina envy.

•

So after Ela's pupils have not been seen for hours and her body is jerked by spasms from head to toe, and men no longer know where their cocks end and her cunt starts, after they have cried enough tears and have poured into her their last lifedrops, men groan with stunned, paralytic grief, dash forward in paroxysm and shrivel inside her. But they refuse to withdraw and face the deflated world outside of her. Instantly, her wondrous cunt swells around them, so that even after the men droop dizzy from defeat, they still fit tightly in her cunt and can sense it resurrecting them; and then they hear her deep reverberant laugh.

•

Sometimes Ela feels she has exhausted her cunt's inventiveness that previously unlocked her as a wind into the world. The sex that gave her freedom, seems old. She feels doomed to repeat herself. But only sex can contain her inner seismic turbulence and make the anxiety of being herself something she can laugh at.

4. DEATH: EPILOGUE

People behave outrageously with Ela, for they need to give themselves to her, but also to find a respectable reason for their spontaneous subjugation. They treat her everyday actions as proof of her love for them. 'Don't be afraid of your love! You can fool yourself, but you can't fool me!' they claim.

•

Ela counsels her followers: 'I am not necessary to you. I am the light from a thigh suddenly revealed under a lifted dress.' When Ela tells her followers that they stifle her, they offer to take her away from this world that drains her. The idea of her rescue, of saving her from others, becomes the centre of their lives.

•

As Ela lacks common sense, she needs friends or servants to look after her. But being served by people who love her is exhausting and keeping those who serve her from loving her is impossible. That is the deadlock of Ela's quotidian existence. It explains the high turnover of all the persons who are connected to her.

•

Men don't think Ela is subject to need, disease or growth; they don't believe she had a past, or a childhood. In her presence, words become cumbersome and meanings fall apart. She seems like a vision that may vanish at any moment. Men blab: 'Women like you turn up in literature, they can't sit across the table and eat dinner with me!' 'You are life to me, but it's strange to be near you!' Ela responds: 'How sad that I am everything to you.'

•

No one knows who Ela is. So everyone wants her. 'This is the real thing,' men think, and want to rise up to her standards. She embodies everyone's ideals and pretences, for she is arbitrary, like a dream-condensation; that is her freedom.

•

Ela's freedom is mere indifference. She lives well on her indifference, for people love her freely and easily because her own affections are not involved. They feel proud to possess her unpossessed spirit and to buy her all that she can do without.

•

People exist as fiction for Ela. The world is a second language for her. She contemplates: People can't see that I am normal. No one presumes that I am a subject. I need a sign on me.

•

Men endlessly develop florid theories about Ela. They assume she contains more than meets the eye and undertake to unveil her. 'Behind Ela's confidence beats a heart wounded by a fatal love for a man,' some judge. 'If you solve me,' Ela contends, 'I am not a mystery. If I am a mystery, do not solve me; make up your mind.'

•

Ela thinks: Love is a curse. Don't be loved and you'll be happy.

•

'Oh, Ela,' men babble, 'I'd be happy if I could just look at you across the table for the rest of my life!' Every man whom Ela meets advises her: 'You must become the real you. No one knows you like I do. You must get to know yourself. The real you is sensitive, sweet, insecure. Let me impregnate you.'

Amidst such emoting, Ela's life would be terribly trite if she didn't have the mirror. As it is, she looks into it and thinks: I live in a playground and I have a clown's face! What fun!

5. BIOGRAPHICAL POSTSCRIPT

Ela grew up in a secluded mansion with vaulted, hand-painted ceilings and cool shiny tiles. Her family owned villages, villagers, animals, huts and acres of land. It took pride in its nine centuries of pure blood, although intermarriage took its toll.

Her maternal grandfather was the High Priest of the Coptic Church, bishop and godhead, reputedly the most handsome man in the nation, magnificent in his flowing gold robes and biblical beard. His large piercing eyes, pale lips, soft fingers, tall powerful body and talent with words of any kind made him a lady-killer. Before God called him to His path via a recurrent macabre vision (his castration by nuns), he was a narcissist and a bisexual playboy. As proof of his conversion to Christianity, he married his only cousin, Penelope, a meek, God-fearing creature who bore him nine children, all of whom died but the last: a tiny girl whose premature birth finally killed poor Penelope.

Grandfather played the organ in church so divinely that tears flowed from the eyes of all who listened. Crowds flocked to hear him sing hymns in the voice of the old Sirens. He found a miraculous fragrant icon of the Pink Virgin in a hot spring on the day Ela was born, led by another blinding vision; he built a cathedral on that spot in the Virgin's honour. Pilgrims brought Her mounds of silver votive puppets. She specialised in curing the blind. Her portrait, done in mosaic, decorated the holy sanctuary. Ela had posed for the baby Jesus held in Her arms.

Ela's paternal grandmother, Penelope's sister, had sold her soul to a moneylender and then stolen the contract. She'd married and murdered nine rich men of various nationalities and amassed a vast fortune. She led the Resistance in both wars, took thousands of lovers, ran in the national elections on her own ticket and, if it wasn't for the peasant majority, would have won. She was famous for her charity, her terrifying tantrums, and for being the most sexually active woman of her class. She had frightening green eyes, a biting tongue, a tremendous hunger for everything, an iron will and disarming charisma. Ela was named after her.

Ela's father was a passionate irresponsible artist who sacrificed a promising career, and a famous string of European mistresses, to live in isolation with the wife his revered mother arranged for him in order to preserve the familial purity and longevity. He wore torn overalls, drank wine and cognac all day and loved to eat and dance. He was hairy, tanned, muscular, bare-chested, affectionate and spent his time developing photographs.

Ela's mother was an otherworldly, self-contained, virginal girl who had no interest in the world outside her room, and no activities other than singing, bathing and resting. She wore exquisite gowns every day, was never in the sun, had impeccable, intricate manners, ate sparingly, spoke rarely and fainted daily. Technically, she had died at birth, but she was resurrected in her coffin three days later, after Grandfather locked himself inside his church and threatened the Virgin that he would set himself on fire if She did not deliver a miracle. Thus Ela came to be born.

Young Ela was given absolute gratification. No rules were placed upon her. But she abstained from worldly pleasures and spent her days in the seclusion of the best possible world: life happened in her head. She had no patience for the surrounding forests, orchards, streams, the pure-bred horses, the ancestral traditions or her tutors. Daily life revolved around her as comedy. She was lauded as the gift from heaven. Dad called her a jewel, a miracle, his life's joy, his only hope, the familial *raison-d'être*. She suspected a grand elaborate trap hid behind his words. The trap was the world. The bait was love.

Had she believed in their words, she would have become a mere idol. But she resisted, preferring to make herself into the most lonely of creatures: a creator. From early on, the simplicity and passion of other people bewildered her. Their endless fussing over her, and her own caressed and protected little body, displeased her. Hundreds of peasants came to offer her ritual blessings, predict her fate, bury her in flowers and kiss her feet every day. Her birthday was celebrated with exorbitant fiestas, when locals were so honest in their joyous worship of her that she assumed they expressed the sentiments of all humanity.

Ela never knew that she was a child. She was a tiny, well-dressed girl with burning eyes and tangled hair, who was prone to ecstasies, had the final word in all family decisions, and asked those she met if they knew God's true face or if they knew how to fuck. She was impatient to have sex, but, despite her demands, no servant dared humour her, for fear of God. She recited Coleridge at four. At six she fell in love with Rimbaud. At nine, with Gertrude Stein. After that, she lost all interest in words.

Squatting in the dark for hours, young Ela created a world more exciting than the one outside her: she flew across the sky, her suitors hanged themselves from trees; islands, rocks and seas called out her name in need, and she emerged out of nowhere in flowing scarlet veils and killed in one blinding blow a thousand savages. She thought with elation: 'I am All and I am Nothing; I am the Fear of fear, the Ruler of destiny, the Destroyer of fact! I require no one else for my happiness. I am alone through eternity, for I remain free for ever. If the universe tumbles down around my ears, what is that to me? I am the peace.'

When Ela was nine, her family was forced to flee to Europe, persecuted by one of those blind fits of nationalism to which Arabs are prone. They ran for their lives in secret, leaving 900 years of history behind to be confiscated by the mob. No longer the centre of a vast fortune, a venerable name and an adoring population, Ela suddenly became an anonymous foreign entity who had to compete and survive in a vulgar world. She had only been trained in the exercises of the imagination. But now she required pedestrian skills, secular weapons and foreign languages.

She was shocked to meet other children. Ela abhorred their primitive groups that shared the same jokes, games, enemies and preoccupations. The democratic chaos of school – with smart, slow, clean, dirty, big, small, meek, mean, ugly, pretty, rich and poor students piled together and subjected to common rules – struck her as ludicrous and incomprehensible. But alienation, Ela's family heritage and her natural mode of being, was an insult if it was imposed from outside; so she had to abandon it.

Ela's humiliation: on her first day in school, there was an excursion to an olive grove on a rocky hill. During tag-and-freeze an ugly boy chased her. She ran fast, cursing her untrained, pampered body. He caught her with a smirk; his thick fingers and dirty fingernails touched her on the left breast. According to the rules, Ela froze on the spot under a deformed olive tree.

She realised then that the world was full of nonsensical regulations and she vowed never again to share the laws of the masses. Aware of a burning hole between her legs, she spent that hot afternoon in defeat: a woman turned into a pillar of salt.

She ran home to the mirror and made faces into it. Her mirror showed her that she was a surprised abyss who to everyone else was a surprised angel; that she would never jump at the sight of her shadow; that she needed no excuses. She wrote with lipstick on the mirror: 'The world will never know me', 'The world is too small for me', 'I will fool the world, and it will make me into a saint'. That day she switched from thumb-sucking to a mature addiction: masturbation. It was her new act of freedom.

The next day in school she lurched into speech as a woman dying of thirst dives into the mirage of an oasis. The correct words came out of her mouth without hesitation or zeal. Her public moments were inspired delaying tactics for self-preservation, comic manoeuvres designed to stay her terror as she rebelled against her needy new world. She prevailed by her innate cockiness as an heir apparent; and she suffered as any actress.

Ela's spoiled body betrayed her in school: she caught colds, children's diseases; she didn't run, jump or aim adequately. Her body was a burden, an obstacle. Her frailty separated her from the others; she felt like a message trapped in a bottle at sea.

She persuaded her classmates that their physical activities were absurd; as a result, her class failed P.E. *en masse*. She led a boycott of the national holiday parade on the grounds that the PM whose refusal of the Nazis' ultimatum was celebrated was himself a Fascist responsible for the deaths of countless democrats. The protest became an annual tradition in the capital, though Ela's initiative was born from her terror of marching in line.

Her male teachers fell in love with her even though she was only ten. They held her hand, cried on her lap, told her their secrets and begged her to run off with them. The female teachers tried to pass on to her the wisdom of lives wasted as good daughters, wives, mothers and patriots. The schoolgirls imitated Ela's ways and ruthlessly competed to serve her. The boys followed her in troops, slept on her doorstep, accused and injured one another or themselves in desperate macho feats meant to impress her. Her name was carved on every tree and every desk. Older high-school boys scrawled 'Ela I love you' on their arms with knives and ran to show her the bleeding incisions. They wrote on the city walls in huge black signs: 'I LOVE ELA' and 'ELA: I AM YOURS!'

The admiration of the crowd did not penetrate Ela. They love me, she thought, feeling nothing of it. They know that it won't come to any good, but still they give themselves over to me. There is more of me than this, she thought as she saw them coming to her. She saw no image of herself in the world. At ten, Ela had already formulated her basic approach to people:

1 Show them love, appear open and remain opaque.
2 Never believe what they say. (I don't know how to believe.)
3 Have no sympathy for easy victims and take no prisoners.

For fun, she practised hallucination. She saw a rowdy brothel in place of a Byzantine church, an immense phallus held by screeching griffins on the Liberty statue, a family of fat hermaphrodites involved in a complex orgy during maths class, centaurs galloping on the city highways with their manes loose in the wind or a pink bubbly parlour at the bottom of her teacup. As long as life was not real, life gave her joy and solace.

Late at night, she crossed alone the wide, silent boulevards inhaling deep breaths of freedom and libido, feeling that she was the maker of everything she saw. She squeezed under the wires and into the ancient ruins to lie on the hot rocks. She peered into every lit window. She knelt and stared into the basements of the poor. She watched sailors argue in bars, gypsies bellydance in their camps, drag queens bargain their asses in the square, tired whores sit with rippled open thighs on top of steep staircases, ghostly nightclub singers eat lamb soup at dawn, calm opium users share pipes at the outskirts of the forest and, deep in the forest, young couples perform rape or love. She hid from cops, cabbies and kind-hearted strangers. She learned to move silently, see and hear sharply, judge fast. Those she saw became characters in her fantasies. She felt her 'subjects' love her through the mist of her imagination; with a love that gave her space and solitude.

She imagined what her subjects thought, desired, concealed. Their acts gave unpredictable directions to her stories. Her new fantasies were live! She saw girls give birth to stones or hogs, a massive underground factory that churned out fake humans, and surveillance insects patrolling the sky. She warned no one of it.

Soon Ela became a familiar figure of the night, greeted by men exposing themselves behind the bushes, their eyes glowing in the shadows with triumph, lust and fear; as she stopped to watch their plight, they bowed to her and jerked off. She befriended queens who hustled for tickets to gay conventions, fled from the sirens and strolled on the cobbled pier where soccer players ran after them, attacking their shaved asses like pastries.

She joined anarchist activists and leftist parties, spied on nuclear arms and political prisoners, covered the city monuments with illegal slogans and posters, wrote soul-searching songs with old men drinking grappa beyond the curfew hours. She enjoyed the meaninglessness of politics – the endless labyrinths of words that were never penetrated by the light of the outside world. She loved the arrests, the handcuffs, the bloated guards, the orange uniforms, and the forlorn parasites who lived in the prisons.

When Ela was twelve and had just been elected school president, she first discovered that dancers, acrobats or construction workers could give her profound physical pleasure. She dedicated herself to developing her cunt. It was the most exciting time. She changed partners like panties, or like words. Every time the lights went on, she found herself with a new lover trying out a new position. She did not suspect then that the overflooding in her cunt might one day become redundant, nor that she could not survive for ever with a bottomless cunt she couldn't understand or control. She loved her new rootlessness. The world was a live show produced for her delight. Her life was not different from dreaming awake. Let the waters part, she winked at the mirror, for Ela has won the Eternal Cunt! May her Wheel of Fortune spin for ever! She went around the world in search of release . . .

HOW SHE LOST IT

Ela is walking up and down the street, lost in herself. An old wrinkled man comes towards her and expertly thrusts his hand under her long dress between her thighs. It feels like a *déjà vu*. Ela's disoriented shock is tempered by the nostalgic pleasure of trying to locate the familiarity of his gesture.

She looks up at the world with quick indignation, or so she hopes; she is unsure of the correct facial expression one would wear in response to this invasion. Is there a customary cry of irritation or horror that she should utter? Should she frown?

Ela finds it absurd to be possessive of her wayward cunt, but she wants to show that she disapproves of the grandfatherly stranger's uninvited handling. *Andante*, she tells herself.

I'm such a thief, Ela thinks, feeling herself act as if she has made up or as if she owns her gestures, feigning surprise at the flaming doves flying out of her sleeve. Nothing of me that others see belongs to me. I reveal what I have stolen. *Largo.*

It is a pleasure for any passing spectator at this moment to look into Ela's eyes as they mirror the daylight with exaggerated amazement and an undercurrent of coquetry. Falseness becomes her. The spectacle tantalises passersby, who turn to gape.

She is wearing a head-dress of silver ostrich feathers that rise above her head and fall down the back of her black gown of a crêpe de Chine tunic sheathed in iridescent veils with pointy sleeves trailing from her wrists. She rises so majestic in her labyrinthine dress that her head seems to touch the sky; so elegant that she makes everyone around her feel inadequate.

Pedestrians stop dead in their tracks. They look eager to egg on the old man or take bets on the fight; for, despite her disadvantageous circumstances, Ela looks like she is the one who gives the orders. These sightseers glance at one another for a validation of the authenticity of the assault. Once they ascertain that this is a bona fide mystery, the spectators take up positions to watch the rising action. They resemble people who assured themselves of a good view in a triumphal procession by camping on the grounds the night before. They are the *hoc genus omne*. They see themselves as stagehands in the unfolding drama.

Looking at the naive mob standing around her like a class of students impatient to learn, Ela secretly knows that she has only her cunt to blame for her present crisis. It is the old trouble with her cunt. It inspires senseless behaviour. Ela doesn't feel responsible for what happens to it. Only minutes ago, as she took it for a stroll to distract its hunger, she felt it open and shut its rims and quiver rapidly like a telegraph wire sending out an urgent code. Ela wonders: My cunt writes my story. What gives it such power? Where does it come from? 'Did he who make the lamb make thee?' Who is in control? This cunt or I? Is 'it' I?

Meanwhile the old man has a knife in his big primitive hand that is now groping between her thighs. He does not look up. He busily faces down at her cunt, oblivious to Ela, bent over with a grimace of single-minded concentration that distorts his face into countless thin, dry lines. He squints like a surgeon performing a delicate operation. He may be holding a surgical tool. He bites his lip solemnly, like a boy dissecting his first fly.

In suit and tie, impeccably manicured, smelling of Ivory soap, Ela's violator appears to have come from a conservative masculine world with bottled ships on spacious desks and leather-bound encyclopaedias. He looks like he collects solid eighteenth-century English oak, Ruskin watercolours and Flemish prints. He wears a dignified 18K. handcrafted Raymond Weil Fidel-co watch on his left wrist. Smallpox pits mark his grey, leathery skin. His breath is so hot and thick it clouds her eyes as they roam his face. Ela thinks: This aggressor belongs by a Blüthner piano. *Larghetto.*

Ela gazes down at his high tapering forehead, the severe brows, the lowered eyes, the hawk-like bridge of his nose, the cracked lips drawn firmly together, his blue clean-shaven cheeks that reflect the light. A sweet melancholy odour emanates from him; its sweetness contains the essence of death. She feels the hankering tingle of her cunt; she casts him as the romantic lead.

She recalls an ageing eye surgeon who slept with her last week and then ran home and killed his son with a kitchen knife, because he wanted no ties outside her cunt. Is this her *déjà vu?*

The sober old man locks his fingers on the rims of Ela's cunt and pulls at it with force as if trying to detach it; as if it were glued on her like an optional attachment, a gadget.

This reminds Ela of her first public sexual experience. Dressed in riding pants, a burned Maoist T shirt and a Cretan knife in her belt, her arms wrapped in hospital gauzes to escape PE, ten-year-old Ela was walking up the dark avenue of Democracy when she had felt something alive on her cunt. An adolescent with feverish eyes, a new moustache and an 'available for mass consumption' macho expression, his shirt buttoned low to expose abundant chest hair and a fat gold pendant, had expertly unzipped her pants, and his cold fingertips which, she imagined with joy, reeked of tobacco and sweat, pulled at the rims of her cunt.

Ela had been amazed by the transformation on the boy's face as he probed: he became gentle, grateful, almost intelligent. He shut his eyes, fell on his knees as in prayer and said: 'Where did you get this gem?' Was it an epiphany? His eyes looked wet and unfocused. Her cunt became wet. He rummaged her tiny cunt with his tongue which felt like a home-made sausage or a mouse, and gave her a miniature orgasm. Ela thanked him with a courteous dip of her head, pulled up her pants and took off. When she looked back, he was still kneeling on the kerb in stupefaction. She realised then that her greatest desire was to become God.

It is autumn. Things are dying. The colours are turning red. It is a time of indecision, emasculation and warmth. It is the perfect time for Ela, who feels herself neither alive nor dead.

For the benefit of her audience, Ela's face now displays the electric pallor of a storm, her eyes the dimness of breathed-on glass. Her hair, loosened by the initial violence, looks like the nest of unknown insensitive birds or an alien napping in mid-air; it forms two silver wings that rise upward and back. She holds herself peacefully: only the quiver of her lips betrays the incessant machinations and hullabaloo of her cunt. *Moderato.*

Ela isn't certain if she owes it to her audience now to make up her mind and put up a fight. Should she call loudly for help? Some observers look perplexed; they must wonder whether to save her at the risk of being slashed or to sit back and enjoy the free show and their guilt, with a hot dog or pretzel purchased from the moustached Mediterranean vendor who stands prominent among them in his stained white apron and oversized sneakers.

But her protest might deflate her enraptured attacker, who is now quivering undisturbed between her legs, and it might force him to retreat before she or the audience have a clearer notion of his motives and aspirations. And wouldn't the audience prefer to have the enigma prolonged? Aren't they favourably disposed to dark suspense? September, after all, is the perfect month for mysteries.

Ela takes off her sunglasses, exposes her immense eyes to the world and stretches out her neck, like Mallarmé's faun imploring in a dead tongue, in a pose that drives vampires and executioners mad. Her gaze unnerves the crowd, who shift about.

Ela has her familiar sense that she is outside of life, an onlooker; that the spectators are the actual partakers of life. She thinks: My mind is the result of being harassed. What seduces me into action? Is life a mute expression of the incomprehensible?

....

'Oh, oh, I'm an alien, I'm an illegal alien, in NY . . .'

....

A light flashes in Ela's eyes, in response to the burning in her effulgent cunt. Her cheeks are gay and her lips moist. The rising vaginal pain sharpens her senses to the keenness of red hot steel. She wants to tilt the sunlight and direct the rays along her assailant's outstretched arm to catch a glimpse of the blade that she now feels so active inside her. *Forte.*

She watches the old man's shuddering and ritualistic rise and fall as if recording the world's maladroit struggles. The bright cars moving behind him seem part of another world, as if rolling on a 3D videoscreen in the background.

The light changes. Ela is bleeding now. The blood has attracted a larger motley crowd of shopowners and shoppers. They feel nostalgic for the genuine dignified pre-war crimes of passion; the old irrational romantic acts of the heart. Alienation is transparent, Ela thinks as she watches them. *Mezzo forte.*

With such great expectations, the crowd grows so extensively that people arriving at the back, crane their necks expecting a stand-up comic, a preacher or a pantomime; they wait for the round of applause at the end of a routine when the audience will disperse, and they can move in. Some search their pockets for change.

Crowds always love to pry into Ela's secrets, for latent in even her most stagy gesture is an indifference to consequences: she has no interest in running from Herod's knife. Her insolence cuts through everyone's cocoon. She gives her spectators the impression that they are watching a sight so rare that it makes them worthy of being themselves watched by another audience; she enables the world to feel watched, and needed, like a celebrity.

The cunt, the main attraction hidden by the curtain of Ela's dress, is wet; aroused by its attacker's impenetrability even more than by his groping. He doesn't strut or fret. He files away at Ela's cunt like a prisoner patiently sawing at his cell bars.

Ela's inspiring cunt is being butchered. The aged Vandal is resolved to get to the root of it. Seconds pass. He stabs at her cunt, murmuring: 'You fucking godless cunt!' *Sotto voce*.

Ela is intrigued by his soliloquy. He sounds firm. Can he be mistaking her for someone else? Should she ask him? But, knowing the intimidating effect of her husky accent, she refrains from speech until she can better appreciate the scene. She thinks: My cunt is my gag; it prevents any other communication.

The sky lowers perceptibly. Ela feels herself enlarging. But as a typical Mediterranean she is less interested in her own precarious fate than in the intimate affairs of those around her. She can't help wondering: What role is he playing? Why did he choose me? Am I the representative of all women in his eyes or is it specifically my cunt that he is punishing? Is he an archetype? Is he serious? Is this an experiment? A necessity? Is it common practice? Is there a proper name for this activity? Is there a big picture, a plot, a pact behind it? Does he have an erection? I can't see. Can the crowd see? *Capriccioso*.

The crowd thinks: Is she paying him for this? Is she getting paid for this? Is it a 9 to 5 job? Can I bring my friends here some time? Is it street theatre? Why is it for free?

Ela thinks: I can see him fucking: raping the lock, treating his cock as a key. Everybody comes: death is the first and final argument. My cunt is nothing to me. Show it to me. *Allegro.*

At this instant, bleeding and feeling faint, Ela is suddenly experiencing the so-called joy of life: something is happening! Perhaps she was made for this world after all! There is surprise in life! She suddenly feels towards this man the soft affection that she feels for her crystal ancestor: her old faithful mirror that is her link to herself and her only worldly attachment.

'She sees something,' an eyewitness gushes. Dozens of eyes open wide. The masses crave a religious experience. Ela dilates her pupils, rolls them up into her skull, and then gazes directly at the onlookers one by one until they feel certain, as if a chasm is opening around each one of them, that they are fraudulent, alone, facing an ice-cold mirror. They feel a new fear, far greater than the fear of death; the fear that they are dreaming. Some look around them for a quick getaway, maybe food or a beer. They twitter, turning to each other, moving closer together. She thinks: They're surrendering to me. *Vivere pericolosamente.*

It all suddenly makes sense to her: this old man has pride. Her cunt is being penetrated in places it has never been touched before. Her proud cunt is now permanently marked by this man. He is planting himself inside her like an olive tree. *Spiritoso.*

She senses the knife, the device, hot and mechanical, slicing into her. Her inflamed cunt sizzles like drenched embers. She thinks: This is the Man as originally scripted: he doesn't beg, flatter, whine, trick; he trespasses. This man can kill my parents, my past, my image. He doesn't seek refuge in metaphors; when he must have my cunt, he doesn't say: 'I'll rip your cunt off'; he does it. Here, in front of the old Frick museum. *Con brio.*

She remembers that last night a lover read to her an article about a young Japanese couple: the man ate his girlfriend and the cops found left-over steaks of her in his fridge. The man said it was the ultimate consummation of their love; she had consented to it. She had demanded: 'Eat me.' This is the sort of reality Ela can understand naturally, without feeling stupid.

Her black dress unfolds like a stage backdrop, as Ela leans over her morose slasher like a wide-spreading vampire opening up to swallow him. He shudders visibly. She presses on his tense shoulders with her small hands, reassuringly. *Rallentando.*

Attuned to his jabs, alert to the moment, Ela feels that she is living at last! She senses his blazing effort, the danger of their public union. Together they are doing irreparable damage: they are uprooting the despotism of her cunt. She has never before tasted such total freedom. *Crescendo.*

She thinks: I am not imagining this.

The crowd thinks: Is it love?

The sky is slowly coming down on them. Ela stands relaxed and receives each sure-handed thrust with a deep inhale.

Now the vaginal pain shoots through her as if to wake her up, and she thinks: I am a virgin at last. *Sforzando.*

....

'I made it through the wilderness, I didn't know how lost I was, I was sad and blue, but you made me feel shiny and new, like a virgin, touched for the very first time, like a vu-u-ur-gin . . . with nothing to hide . . . my fear is fading fast, till the end of time . . .'

....

Despite having the world's tightest cunt, Ela never before bled and assumed that she was born ready for intercourse, or else that she had not been adequately pierced yet. This is the first sexual act that doesn't reconfirm to Ela that men are inadequate.

Now Ela finally understands what men mean when they ooze in her ear: 'My cock is a knife cutting through you, coming out of your mouth, opening you up!' She had never felt any such knife going into her. Now she no longer has to live in metaphor: this man's knife makes a difference. It makes her aware of herself.

Shreds of flesh and clots of blood splatter Ela's thighs. Tiny pink streams slither down her legs. In her brain, a child soprano sings: '*Blood has flowed, honour is saved . . .*' *Arioso*.

The crowd does not have to look up to see the sky, for it now envelops the action like a narrator's voice. The clouds drift through Ela's legs in haloes. Everyone present is startled by this stark intimacy between the elements. *Veloce*.

Ela thinks: I have been a mistress of disguise, and at this moment I am finally being discovered. I open like a bud.

It is an experience she is not to attain again: Ela feels loved. For an overburdened instant, she knows in her bones that this man loves her. She can believe it: someone loves her! This new, awkward emotion spreads out like carbon monoxide inhaled by all present; it gives her a migraine immediately.

Are these, then, the dreaded symptoms of reciprocal love? Is some unavoidable putrid-smelling gangrene spreading through Ela's body? Love flutters in her lungs, swells up against her diaphragm, burns and upsets her stomach. It is an impersonal, secretive force that presses at her insides and chokes her. Her stomach cannot digest her toxic love. Her organs resist. Her virginal heart falters. She wants to puke. The clouds dance around her. Her heart is a black clay pot forgotten on the fire.

So on this NYC corner, Ela stands lovestruck, like a lost ghost trapped in a confusing respect for another being. I'll die of love, she thinks, I am in the midst of the unadulterated butchery of love! Ela relishes the blows of her love, as St Barbara must have relished the infidels' tortures with divine exuberance.

A smouldering scent of rotting apples spreads in tidal waves around her. The crowd experiences the first pangs of its emancipation from the petty bookkeeping of ordinary existence. It feels like breaking into an impromptu rendition of '*When the Saints . . .*'

Ela thinks: Love is my rite of passage, I must face it. If I love, I am no longer trapped in being me. This is my chance to be possessed; to Die. For a deceptive instant, Ela no longer sees death as her reason to live but as the mirror: a blonde garbed in gold dust, who smokes, sways her lazy hips, and is so civilised she has done away with all language, down to the last word: Come.

With Ela's first sigh of love, the world feels lighter and dizzy, like during take-off aboard a flimsy plane. *Affettuoso*.

At that same instant, the man wavers and falls to his knees, exhausted and panting like a regimental standard-bearer. Yet he persists with his cunt-chopping, like a starving woodpecker, or a Cuisinart gone berserk. As one cycle of pain ends, a new wave of passion is immediately generated that sends Ela's senses climbing again in a single breathless movement to the very summit of life.

The fallen man grabs her knees for support. She is seized by sympathy. By now the sky has dropped so low that she is shrouded in ominous clouds; it makes her feel claustrophobic.

In the amber light, her love looks at least a hundred years old. He exhales cold gusts of air. He wheezes like a dying man.

Yet he keeps cutting. She runs her pale fingers through his hair tenderly, as if to encourage or to cherish him. Her ring gets caught in his sparse tufts. She jerks her finger away but she only manages to uproot a handful of dry white hairs. The knots around her ring are so complex that she has to use both her hands to disentangle her trapped finger. This takes a few seconds. In the course of that affectionate moment she hears his faint sobs, a sad blend of muffled whimpering and suffocation.

She is also struck by:

(a) her beloved's face is distorted into unsightliness as tears well from beneath his dreamer's straight white lashes and brim over into a glistening stream that wets her exposed thighs;

(b) the eyeball on her ring, a glass eye of the kind blind people insert in their empty, wrinkled sockets in order to appear to see, an old amulet given to Ela by a witch on MacDoughal who strangled herself with her own hands because Ela could not love her back, is suddenly staring up at her as if questioning her;

(c) a macabre novel written years before by her third-best lover and dedicated to her, titled *The Blind Knife*, a love story that Ela did not understand then, comes back to her now, out of the caves of her memory, and strikes her as suddenly relevant.

The onlookers push forward inquisitively with glittering eyes and thick wool jackets reminding Ela of a cluster of fleecy cattle. But, for now, Ela has forgotten about her herd.

Ela locks her palm on the stranger's chin, gently pulls up his face toward her and studies it closely, upside down. She sees his pouting purple lips, his swollen brown gums, his few stained ochre teeth, his overflowing saliva; his streaked sunken cheeks, his thick ashen stubble, his corroded sockets, his white empty eyes. A milky, spotty film like rancid cum covers his eyeballs.

Ela thinks: This man has cum coming out of his eyes!

Looking into this despondent masque, Ela feels inclined to vomit. Her man wears the tacky, permanently imploring expression of Christ-being-taken-off-the-cross idols. He has the broken, flaccid, slow-witted, nauseating beauty of a Pietà. *Diminuendo*.

She mindlessly lets go of his head, and it drops lifelessly on his chest. The knife, the senseless prop, stays busy. The cuts come softer, sloppier inside her. The blind man sighs like a rookie cop who must alone disassemble a ticking bomb. *Tremolo*.

Ela thinks: A blind man is destroying my cunt! What a buffoon! I was not chosen! This was a random act! How did he even know I was a woman? It is all an innocent mistake. A misunderstanding. I thought he'd unmask me, but it is himself he unmasks; that always happens. She feels a restless, skin-tight disgrace. She feels her cunt in her mouth. She swallows hard.

Suddenly Ela hears her grandmother's hiss in her ear: 'Stay away from the blind, for they see in the dark. They can see us. I am not allowed to say any more about it. The rest you must find out on your own. Beware!' So her grandmother had warned Ela years ago as she lay dying. Ela had assumed that the advice was metaphorical. Now she thinks: It is too late. I can't prescribe what happens next: I don't see the overall picture. I have been fooled. I let myself be part of someone else's plot.

By now the gloomy affected sky lies on her feet disembowelled.

Out of courtesy to her audience, Ela resists her impulse to faint. The crowd! she remembers, the crowd I am forever fleeing from and fleeing to: the big, inarticulate stimulant. She thinks: I still pitch to the crowd. I am still a hoax. It's OK.

She thinks: I haven't lost it yet. I could sew it up.

The old man thinks: What was Homer's connection to Helen? What was his reward? How could he survive without seeing her?

She thinks: My core is now being cored.

The old man thinks: Did Homer invent Helen's beauty? Was Helen a hag? Was his epic work his revenge upon the seeing?

Ela thinks: Is this a game of blind man's bluff?

....

The mirror thinks: Is it my fate to never be seen? I have the solution to this plot snag: turn the camera on me.

....

A vainglorious twilight is setting in. Things turn bloody, before they disappear. In this dimmed light, death feels so close that for a split second Ela has to think of wet poppies or a girl's panties forgotten on an old wooden table or fat mothers smiling on sunlit balconies, in order to open up some space for herself to breathe in. At this breathless alarming hour the world seems hanging by a thread, like a lover just about to come.

The crowd pales and shivers with anticipation. *Lacrimoso.*

Now once again, Ela cannot but fall prey to herself: this man wanders in the streets with dead eyes, she thinks. So do I. What distinguishes me from someone blind is a conjuring trick: I can pretend to see. It is assumed that my eyes connect to my brain, as it is assumed that only one girl lies in the magician's coffin and is sawn in half. This man wants to conquer my cunt. So do I. And staring at my cunt so intently could blind anyone. It blinds me all the time. We are in this together. Partners.

Here lies a man who can't see me; a man I can see without being seen; a man I see not seeing me. A man I cannot pose for. His blank eyes show me that I do not exist. In his eyes, I am in a reversed exposure. Free from human gravity. Here lies a man who may never have looked in the mirror. A man that pure!

Ela performs the most instinctive – blind – act of her life: she leans over protectively and rests her palms on the backs of the blind man's rough, wet, knobby hands. She closes his fingers tightly around the knife. Adjusting to the rhythmic movements of the man under her, she adds all her strength to the thrusts. The knife goes berserk. She closes her eyes and notices how expertly each return of the blade stabs at the contours of her cunt in the quickest, deepest and least painful way possible. *Staccato*.

The two pairs of hands obsessively rise and fall under her dress that is by now pulled far above her naked thighs. Everyone is concentrating on what lurks under the big black dress. Will flames, pink fluffy rabbits or chubby white doves leap out of there? Or will the rabbits come out strangled and skinned, the doves carved and skewered, the flames liquid like blood?

The knife hits Ela's rich central vein. She smiles.

The crowd waits, quietly breathing through their mouths.

Ela realises she is masturbating in front of the mob. Her eyes glitter with challenge. Her rapacious cunt quivers like a fish on land, like a scorpion's tail. Its high seductive death-rattle spreads through her nerves. Her whole body is aflame.

The speechless crowd imagines a tall gallows being set up for Ela at the square and her flesh being branded by fired irons with A for Assaulted; for certainly, at another age, a woman would no doubt have paid with her life for this appalling, frivolous act.

Raw, tiny gasps come into Ela's mouth. Her face is severely white. The pain spreads slowly outward from her depths until her cunt reverberates like the wild clanging of a bell, like 1,000 bells jangling simultaneously at her every breath, rocking her.

She pulls the blade across her flesh. She senses before her the joy of entering a new inexplicable realm, and solving a riddle. She thinks: Is it death I am working towards? Or a wild ecstasy of the senses? The two seem to overlap. *Vibrato*.

The crowd now starts to suspect it is watching an MTV video being shot with hidden cameras, which means they have all been cast to play the involved energetic onlookers gathered at the background to fill the screen. They have been chosen in advance unbeknownst to them, and they'll be approached at the end with a release form to sign and a token payment. Some begin to shake their shoulders and bob their heads to the beat of the stabs. They try not to act self-conscious. Luckily the show is gripping.

The two protagonists push and pull fast. The red evening light flares on them as if they were standing in epic battle.

Now blood spurts from Ela's cunt like a scarlet bird, flying across to the blind man's eye. His crumpled suit is drenched red. His listless skin is parched, like dried mud. His right hand alone is moving, laboriously gripping the slippery knife, hovering shakily like the hand of a marionette. Ela watches his heart-rending, futile exertion, knowing that if it were not for her, the knife would miss its aim. She throws her body at the blade, and the cold steel pierces her cunt, emerging at the other side of it. Her nostrils are assailed by a peculiar smell of vaginal blood. She wants to taste it. It must be sweet.

Her shoulders heave, her eyes are narrow slits, as she feels her cunt vomiting itself out in robust health. Will she come?

Suddenly Ela thinks: Jesus, this is taking a long time. This incongruous thought echoes through her mind and makes her laugh. It is the snappy laughing fit that overtakes Ela during orgasm: an uncontrollable chuckle at the defeat of logic, a hearty cheer at the ridicule of reality, that grows into a demented roaring peal of laughter. Now she giggles flushed and elated, and fights her urge to clap, shout, fling up her head-dress, hug herself, hold her sides and fall on the ground. In the stunned silence, her laugh makes a haunted-house sound: wah-ha-ha-ha-ha! Her body shakes with laughter, her eyes bulge, tears tickle her lowered eyes as she tries to suppress her mirth in vain. *Obbligato.*

The crowd sees her sensitive eyes brimming with shiny tears and thinks that she could be crying. They witness her fierce convulsions and wince, sympathising with her plight.

The blind man, however, who must be oversensitive to mocking sounds, and whose sight can't fool him, collapses on cue like a spent arrow, like a deflated hot-air balloon. *Con dolore.*

Ela cautions herself, still chuckling: Am I elbowing the audience, so high on myself that I pre-empt their response? Isn't this the essence of being an actress: never to apologise?

Realising that laughter in this context is sacrilege, like laughing in church when the priest raises the host, Ela invites sterile thoughts to her head. She ponders: Is this the fall of a man? Is this his tragedy or his triumph? Is he a martyr? How he has aged! No Mac the Knife here. She gloats, feeling heroic like an honourable samurai gutting his abdomen ritualistically.

The collapsed man hangs on to Ela's frame. His limp arms hug her calves, his face is raised toward her like a suppliant's, and he has curled up into a foetal position. He looks like a bled phantasm. Ela draws the heated knife out of his fist with one hand as she strokes her stinging, carved cunt with the other.

Has her blind accomplice died in her arms? It is the due outcome of a fatal love; the closing of the circle. And to stand with a corpse in one's hands is always a powerful experience, an image of grandeur that would not be lost on the audience.

Besides, the old dugout can't take the plot any further.

The crowd is concerned and confused. Who is the victim now? Hesitant simultaneous whispers are uttered: 'Get him help.' 'Get her a chair.' 'Get him under a cold shower.' 'Get an ambulance.' 'Hug him,' a woman urges her. Then, as abruptly as they emerged, the murmurs expire. The audience moves closer, out of an impulse to embrace the two victims, protect and contain them, drawn to them as to two innocent creatures that have fallen from heaven.

Meanwhile, Ela holds the outer edge of the mouth of her cunt and runs the knife around its slashed borders with admiration – expressed by raising her eyebrows – at the clean unobtrusive slits that surround it. She cuts herself as if she were simply peeling a kiwi fruit. She swoons. She shuts her eyes and smoothly slices around the main vaginal walls along the existing incisions, uniting them into one slow continuous circular confident carving.

Gripped in her clenched fist, the five inches of naked point vanish completely into her flesh. Ela senses that each of her labia represents a layer of illusion that must be peeled away before the grave central mystery of life can be revealed. Her chest thumps violently, as in some distant region that she can't believe is a part of herself, an excruciating pain comes welling up. It is as if her cunt has split open to disgorge a boiling stream. A tangible freedom races towards her with terrifying speed. It is a sensation of utter chaos, as if the sky has fallen and the world reels drunkenly. Before her, she sees only a limitless expanse opening out into vast distances. *Legato.*

The mysterious erotic blue hue of dusk overtakes the world like an abruptly lowered curtain, signalling the end of the drama.

The spectators are overwhelmed by sad tenderness. Yet they prevent themselves from rushing to Ela's side: whatever happens, they must watch. That is their duty. That is her trust.

As she pares her cunt out, Ela chants to herself: I want the inside information, the source; I want to know what happens to the things that around me melt like snowflakes, but around everyone else stand solid like monuments. I want to look at it.

I might as well finish this off and see what comes next.

The bystanders on East 70th are presented with a memorable sight: an old man in a grey cashmere suit, black tie and a Panama hat lies bloody and prostrate on the kerb, embracing the naked thighs of a young woman with flowing tall silver plumes and dishevelled silver hair that caresses her radiant face as the wind blows it into sweaty S's, circled unto herself as if in an attempt to unite or rearrange her own spilling vital insides.

And as Ela's cunt drops off, falling with a tiny 'slomp' on the ground, the diverse faces crowding around her are possessed by a unified expression of pity and fear. They all sense that they see something which was never meant to be seen. *Presto.*

The disembodied cunt on the old cracked pavement produces a dreamlike effect on the witnesses of its epiphany. It seems to be burning without being burnt, like Moses' bush. It imparts light.

So it is beauty, Ela acknowledges. The sight of her cunt spreads a white fire of awareness through her nerves. It should not hide all the time, she thinks. Illumination becomes it.

She feels disconcerting, like an irrelevancy. She thinks: Never own anything you can't afford to lose. Losing is liberating. I have freed myself of myself. Here's looking at you, kid!

Her eyes have become absolutely opaque.

....

So Ela and her cunt were not inseparable!

....

In the limelight, the tossed cunt lies simple and complete. It looks indescribably perfect. It has two elegant understated curves coming together. Its frail form gleams like a big dew-drop, an open, vibrant gem in the shape of a circle or a zero. An iridescent viscous film like rose oil covers its skin. Its luminous hue changes endlessly from sea-silver to pearly pink. It catches the eye so irresistibly that one is inclined to search its depths for larger signs of fate, like an ancient crystal ball.

It possesses a texture of inviting furtive softness. Its overlapping porous curves and rich folds are reminiscent of highlighted photos of canyons and sand dunes taken with a 4 × 5 camera.

There is no trace of blood or mark of violence on it. It is miraculously unbruised, even untouched. Perhaps due to its muscle memory, it is lightly pulsing or breathing as in sleep.

No one present can distinguish which exact parts have been carved out, but the result looks excellent: both swollen outer labia are included, the complete erect clitoris, the restless inner labia, and a thin layer of vaginal walls that rises into a cylindrical semi-transparent membrane. No tubes, no uterus, no rectum, no cervix, not a single pubic hair. The Grafenberg spot, probably hidden in the folds, is, as usual, difficult to locate.

Ela is surprised that her cunt does not resemble a beast at all. Despite its shiny surface, it bears no relation to a slug, or a chameleon. It looks inexorable, like any other supernatural being. She thinks: It was not deflowered, but enflowered.

Ela looks at her mutilated cunt and, for the first time, she feels proud of it. Her dress rustles with delicious melancholy. Her skin itches, aroused, her nipples wake up, her veins ripple. The cunt faces her, not mockingly, but curious and observant itself. It seems watchful, vigilant. It stirs as if looking her up and down from head to toes, and appears genuinely surprised.

Ela feels the mutual hellish recognition between them. What seals their new camaraderie is that they like each other. Her incisive gaze makes it quiver. Is this seraphic yawn really her old Quixotic fire-spitting cunt? If I ever love anyone, she now thinks, it will be this evanescent unthinkable water plant. But the last ties between us have just been severed.

There is a clarity, like the clarity of a stream fed from melting snows, in the silence that rests between them. Looking across at her beautiful cunt, Ela is for the first time experiencing true peace of mind. *Dolce*.

The audience is transfixed. People raise a hand to clutch at their hearts but stop halfway, paralysed like butterflies pinned on a mesmerising wall of passion. Through the unfathomable folds, its tiny stinger aims at them like a delicate gun barrel.

The dark red clouds have parted. Cars are passing by, but no sound penetrates the awe of the transported audience. The new star of this street show opens and shuts like a phosphorescent oyster. It could be a deity, Ela thinks, breathing in the centre of an ornate temple, sovereign and benevolent; rituals, perfumes, colours, hopes and hymns should eternally revolve around it.

Is this cunt still considered mine? Ela wonders in euphoria. It surprises her that she doesn't want to leave it behind. Her mind feels knotted, and she misses the sharp puckering of her labia that took place whenever something bothered her: I never thought I would outlive my cunt. What now? How do I live?

She bleeds in thin consistent torrents that drip into tiny pink pools on the pavement. She bends down in slow motion and leaves the bloodstained knife on the kerb next to its victim.

Ela would very much like to sit back now and think of this unusual act as a sacrifice, an immaculate birth, a miscarriage, a joke on men, biology, Shiva's lingam and holy fallen meteorites. But she doesn't have the time. She must leave the stage before the glares of cameras, officers and history catch up with her. She meticulously wipes her bloody fingers one by one on her dress.

A diabolic shadow sweeps over the hundreds of intently watching, terrified spectators. The disenchantment never comes. It is clear that Ela is still wearing several layers of costumes beneath her skin; her nakedness is but a passing manifestation.

The world is full of music, an autumn sadness in its tone.

While the numb stillness lasts, slowly so as not to break the fragile trance, her eyes wide in an aura of dream-freedom, with the intact movement of a girl who tiptoes into her sleeping parents' bedroom or gleans through the diary of an unsuspecting friend or slides out of a sticky body after hours of continuous sex, and with the physical abandon of one who is at home with her body, Ela bends, picks up the indomitable cunt between her thumb and middle finger, places it in her open palm with care, gingerly lets the petrified blind man fall on the ground and takes slow, calculated steps backwards and walks off stage, avoiding any eye contact with the spellbound audience.

As she turns around to leave, she glances up at the whirling dark sky like into a mirrored ceiling, as if to check her face.

The world is soaked in metallic blue hues. Grand clusters of clouds pile upon one another, as if holding out against a dark inchoate force. It seems impossible that a mass so heavy can be borne in the air.

Ela pauses by the stand of the moustached hot-dog vendor and picks up an empty peanut-butter glass jar. She places her hacked plant with reverent gentleness into the jar so as not to destroy the tender roots. This act heightens the confusion of the stupefied audience regarding the nature of the fallen object.

To her own amazement, Ela is fine. She writes to the world on a big banner in her mind: Sorry, I am OK. She quickly strides down the street through the hustling evening crowds, leaving after her the lingering subversive aura of a closed system, and hearing behind her an electrified commotion suddenly explode.

The impulse for violence inherent in every crowd is all at once free to come out. The abandoned spectators behave like freed slaves gathering forces to break into the Colosseum. They all look about with self-importance, make extravagant gestures and impatient facial expressions and ask loud questions: 'What the hell happened, man?' 'Excuse me, sir? Did you see what I saw?' 'What did you see?' 'Don't let her go free!' 'Follow her!' They all search for a leader and all strive to become the leader. In short, they are now a mettlesome, aggravated mob.

Ela ducks into a lavender drugstore and wades through aisles of gleaming, cheap wares. She buys a pack of Super Maxi New Freedom pads and silver-sparkle nail polish. At the counter, a salesgirl in a plaid uniform comments: 'What a bright pretty foetus you have there!' nodding at the jar, while giving Ela her change. A

customer waiting in line affirms: 'I know about being an orphan.'
Ela thinks: The extras are restless, but then, I like it that way.

Ela now dives into a small Pakistani mom-and-pop restaurant.
The odour of burning grease chokes her. She coughs. A tall dark
woman in clogs announces: 'Right this way, Ma'am, your table is
waiting.' She bends forward with the assuring attitude of an old,
dedicated servant, and Ela is tempted to hide in her chest and
refuse to be part to any sequel. The waitress does not glance
at the luminous cunt in Ela's jar. Her eyes are clear and regal,
like a woman's who has no time for men. Bushes of black hair
grow at her armpits. Ela is moved to kiss her. Ela grows faint
from arousal. But the waitress, her face deformed with maternal
worry, hugs Ela's free arm to steady her and, misinterpreting Ela's
sexual signs, delivers her to a purple door marked WC.

Outside, the crowd gathers in circles on the street corner to
practise democracy: everyone speaks but no one is heard. The voices
fight to rise above the clamour: 'The world is unclean!' 'She had a
temper tantrum!' 'Wrong, mister: he had a tantrum!' 'He paid for
it, too!' 'She is definitely a right-brain person.' 'She doublecrossed
him flat out.' 'You call this a happy ending?' 'They'll screw in rivers,
in fields, among a herd of sheep, on the day's catch from the sea, on
our very beds if they get the chance.' 'We're sleeping in a burning
house!' The crowd attracts the attention of cops, who come on the
scene to calm everyone down.

Inside the narrow purple WC enclave, Ela looks in the old
smudged mirror and feels safe. Nothing can hurt her in front of
a mirror. She stares into it for a long time and does not blink,
until her eyes are so bright that they hurt the mirror. It breaks
out into tiny cracks, like struck ice. Ela touches the mirror with
her fingertips, and the sense of the deathly cold skin against the
warmer glass is soothing. *Mezzo piano.*

She is thirsty. She fills the jar with water from the faucet to keep
her cunt moist, and places the jar on the soiled yellow tiles at her
feet. She fans her aching, torn cavity. Then she faints. She regains

her senses and finds herself kissing the filthy floor. She kneels by the toilet. Her joints feel liquid. She cannot control her body. Her jaws rattle. She presses her thumbs against her wrists to stop her circulation and feel numb.

A wave of nausea overtakes her. She takes off her clothes in a desperate fury and falls heavily on to the mouldy cool tiles, abandoning herself to the sickness, washed in cold sweat, noisily flapping from one side to another like a fish on dry ground; as if she were trying to leave her body behind on the floor and take off into thin air. Her insides clamour to come out and a taste of horror settles in her mouth. But after some minutes, when she is cold enough to feel nothing but the goosebumps on her skin, the hyperventilation in her heart freezes down. She sits up with chattering teeth, her skin paler than a vampire's, her gaping wound directly touching the cool grime. She needs to empty herself. She hides her face in the fetid toilet bowl, writhing, grunting, making sounds of throwing up. She sticks her dainty childish finger into her paper-dry throat. Nothing comes out.

There is noise in the restaurant. Ela peeks through a door-crack; she sees two cops. She instantly picks up her cunt jar in her hand like a weapon, sits up on the toilet and gathers her straying wits. She looks down and tells her floating cunt, as she has told many men before, in an intimate tone: 'It was lovely being with you, like sitting on a leaf. But if you knew how hard it is to convince myself that I want you!' She thinks:

1 I should have bought bottled mineral water for the cunt; it may get infected. A small problem, because:

2 The next time any men (including cops) say: 'Give me your cunt, baby,' I can now reply: 'Voilà' and hand it over to them, without becoming personally involved. And:

3 Men can no longer declare in my presence: 'You just can't get rid of that cunt.' That is why:

4 Life is interesting only when metaphors become literal.

But now Ela is trapped in the aftermath: away from the audience, separated from her cunt, she panics. The process by which so fearful an event can melt into everyday life brings on a new fear and fulfilment, as if she has committed a crime that goes undetected. Yet life now seems hollow. *Piano.*

Back in real time, the cops knock on her door. They roar in unison: 'Ma'am are you all right? Can you tell us what happened?'

Ela pees a single drop. She thinks: At least I can still do peepee! A cop: 'Can you understand me? Do you speak English?' The other cop: 'Do you know what date it is?' Cop: 'The 21st.' The other cop: 'Not you! Do you know who is the president of this country? Can you tell me his name?' Ela: 'Rumpelstiltskin?' She thinks: It's not much as personal tragedies go.

Outside, the dark muggy evening is being sprinkled by hard neon lights. There is an ear-splitting silence. *Appassionato.*

On the toilet, Ela fiddles with the tender moist edges of her scissure absentmindedly. She imagines her cunt was a rodent chewing at the root of her, like the elf who saws at the tree of the world, working for the day it could force her to hover over Nothing. All this coring is getting to me, she realises.

Outside The Ironpants Grill, crowds press their faces against the soiled glass door and push angrily against those gathered in front of them. The cops order the restaurant door locked.

Yet the onlookers seem willing to wait. They buy film, buy cameras, pass out business cards, recommend professional women's or abused men's groups, note discount sales, call their shrinks, their agents, Oprah, and suffer secret pangs of stage fright.

A chubby black boy composes a rap on the spot. Petty thieves run busy. Everyone feels like clapping. They feel the excitement of a Miss Marple or an Inspector Clouseau at the scene of an old school chum's ghastly murder. They look sincerely worried, for they assume there is an ultimate matrix common to all people, which of course is why they are members of the crowd.

No one knows if the assailant is still alive, for no one stayed behind to witness his demise. Cops and reporters take notes. There was blood, they are told, torn clothing, a knife; and something fell on the ground, still breathing. A cop reports that the abandoned weapon is missing. Someone took it as a souvenir.

Public excitement is growing. The simmering bystanders perspire. They want to hear her true story. They want to touch her wound which, some remark, has already healed miraculously.

For suddenly a new word of mouth prevails: it was a miracle! A phenomenon of worldwide magnitude! People swear they can see a pair of large prissy red lips like Mick Jagger's up in the sky beckoning to them. Some argue that the miracle is a promotional device. A widespread black woman throbs: 'Soon this site will become a shrine.' A girl in a stretch dress breaks into sobs: 'I missed the whole crime because I had my Walkman on high. Just my luck!' An emaciated man protests: 'Foetuses are living human beings! It was murder! I saw it!' An enthusiastic southerner exclaims: 'I've waited thirty years for this!' *Prestissimo*.

Newcomers emerging out of subways and stores press the crowd for information and, in their ignorance, deepen the mystery: 'Did the corpse levitate?' The Geraldo TV troop arrives with cameras. Reporters call their tabloids: 'BLOODY SATANIC RITE ON 70TH'; 'BLACK MAGIC AT FRICK IN PLAIN VIEW OF THOUSANDS' — first-pager.

Meanwhile, Ela is doing her nails; she applies new coats on the thick silver polish already there. She gropes through her Goofy-faced bag smearing it with wet polish, finds her pack, lights a cigarette: all this in order to concentrate. *Maestoso*.

She remembers she has no panties on. How will she wear a pad to stop the blood trail? She should have bought tampons; but her cavity is too tender from the gutting. She does not want to look down, into her gap. What has she done to herself? What gender is she now? Does she still have an identity, is she a 'she'?

She concludes: I wish I could dream of something. *Grave*.

Outside, the masses are getting impatient. Can the two cops flanking the mystifying WC door hold off the crowd much longer?

The cops: 'Ma'am, we have to see you.' Ela: 'I look fine. Contrary to popular belief, I am just sitting here constipated.'

Her soft voice caresses the vowels; it sensualises the cold, efficient English, giving it curves. Ela thinks: Worse comes to worse, I can walk out singing *Put the Blame On Ma'am, Boys* with open arms; no one would touch me then; but I don't have a glove.

The cop: 'Ma'am, we have to take you away.' Ela: 'A cop's job is to defile.' Both cops: 'Ma'am, we arrested the guy. He won't talk. We need your testimony. We're here to help you.'

Ela tickles the loose shreds of her abdomen absentmindedly. She wonders if she will grow a new cunt. Can she have her old one transplanted? Does she want to? It occurs to her that now she can wear her cunt at will, remove it before sleep, carry it in her purse, lock it in a safe, hang it in the closet, put it in the freezer, heat it up, and, best of all, forget it.

In the jar, now that Ela examines it closer, her cunt looks grotesque: both labia are oversized and colourless, and they move in the water like the suckers of an amoeba. The strong clitoris, situated far too low, points upward and pixillates, like an itchy nose or a searching antenna. Seen horizontally, the silver cunt wears an annoying conceited smirk; a roguish smile that reminds Ela of Iago. Seen vertically, it pouts like the glossy mouth of a sexy vamp. The whole creature looks like an awesome adornment; an overdone embellishment from an alien culture. She takes it out and rests it on her burning palm. She gets gooseflesh.

Then she feels a tight pull on her palm and jumps up with fright, almost throwing the frolicking cunt on the germ-ridden tiles in disgust. The severed cunt just made a leap! It moves! Ela calls out in a high pitch: *'Mommie, it's alive!' Fortissimo.*

As if on cue, an enormous peal of growling thunder invades the toilet. The lights dim. The electric circuits hum. Heaven is crying its eyes out. Ela feels befriended, renewed.

Outside, the placid blue afternoon turns suddenly black, and huge splashes of tropical rain fall like heavy menstrual blood from the sky. It is hard to imagine it ever not raining. The road churns like a frothing river. Fallen blue clouds swirl against the jagged serrations of the high-definition skyscrapers and baroque green rooftops that loom like enormous jawbones. Violent streams tumble down. But despite the deluge pouring from the skies, the inquisitive crowd stays on as drenched sentinels.

Both cops trill: 'Ma'am, we have to break the door.'

Ela drops her cunt in its jar. It now looks like a water spider flashing a spectral light. Ela says: 'That's creepy.' She thinks: I better accept and befriend this accursed alien I've cut out of my body, so that I don't end up like St Augustine running all my life from temptation to civilisation and back.

One cop: 'Ma'am, everything will be all right, once you come out. I promise.' The other cop: 'Do you have a weapon in there?' Ela: 'You leave me no recourse but to surrender so that I can silence you.' She thinks: Cops shouldn't be legal.

She flushes, wipes her vacancy to make sure the bleeding is stopped, pulls her Goofy bag back up on her shoulder and the ostrich feathers on her head. She is attacked by thoughts: How do I throw myself to the hungry crowd? Should I sniff a bit? Let the people pat my shoulder and say: 'I know'? Do I hold my cunt in front of me like a shield? Wear it as a crown and walk out laureled? Hold it between my teeth like the coin the dead bite to bribe Charon for a safe boat journey from one world to the other? Carry it ceremoniously in my raised hands like a holy offering, a chalice, the Gorgon's head, an Oscar? If I use it correctly, I'll be safe. Didn't it hold the masses dead in awe minutes ago? It put me in this precarious position, and it better see me out.

One cop: 'Drop your weapon if you have one, and walk out unarmed.' The other cop: 'We're aiming straight at the door. Don't try anything stupid.' Her cunt glows in the dark.

With her face and cunt uplifted, Ela unlocks the WC door and greets the two cops, who look astounded by her costume and her forbidding countenance: 'I simply had to go to the bathroom. What's with this weather?' The cops tail her, so excited that they feel they should place themselves under arrest. The rain sounds like Jan Garbarek's soprano sax: an enormous bird crying.

Ela walks out under the distraught clouds. She smiles a wide, girlish greeting like a young genius who just completed a concert in the theatre and feels too shy to take a bow. That sweet grin permeates the audience and brings out in them a helpless compulsion for self-expression, a need for sheer noise. The wet crowd murmurs and howls, and suddenly looks like an inviting ocean where Ela can plunge in and be carried away, and may even be reborn.

So Ela dives into the mob as into a cleansing bath. She looks invulnerable like a glowering unworldly eremite with loose, dripping silver hair and eyes like lightning, running crazed out of her cloister into the streets, her ecstatic face like a brilliant white after-image, a wet luminous mask floating in the air.

The multitudes look like children hoping to be molested.

She thinks: I am the clown, I take the pratfalls for them. They have come to watch me get devoured. To strip me, bind me, drag me through the muddy streets, throw me into the flames, then jump in the flames with me; to impale me. I'd like being gored by crowds; to come, for my last time, while penetrated by the stake.

The crowd hesitates. It begs her not to leave, like a crowd of hysterical fans requesting a time-stretching finale from a rock star. They stare and blink, for, out of context, her glittering cunt in the jar could be anything. Their eyes are glazed, like children walking through the fair. No one dares ask: 'Excuse me, Miss, what is it you're holding?' It is an uncomfortable scene: they want to know her inch by inch, to scratch her bare, and then to judge her; but they lack the necessary courage. *Amabile.*

Her surprise attack, and the hard rain that is falling by the bucket, cooling their tempers and forcing them to look for shelter, disarm the onlookers and cancel any sustained plans they might entertain for a violent possession of this elusive duo. They duck imperceptibly and quench their hungry eyes on her. The mob tightens so close around Ela that the pulse from their breasts burns through her veins. She can touch them now. Her unexpected bravery enchants them, like a matador's reckless scientific dance charms the bull. They drip heavily. The contrast between their outer wetness and their inner dry heat is comical.

So the crowd opens up for Ela to cross the street followed by the cops and the roused wet horde. She thinks: This is not a retreat. This is God's orgasm. Everybody duck! *Cantabile*.

But the heavy rainy-day traffic slows down her followers. Anxious drivers rest on their horns and crane their heads out to ogle at the disturbance and ask the cops to keep the crowd off the road. Fist fights erupt. Cops run around, reporters shoot at random, cars are stalled bumper to bumper on the slippery avenue and the crowd is trapped tight in the solid sea of metal.

Ela looks behind her, satisfied, as a person whose epic mission has been accomplished. In the shuffle, she slides down the urine-smelling steps of the nearest subway station, rides the train for three stops, gets off and walks to her building. Success!

A placard marked DEVOTION NEEDS NOT ART – THANK YOU FOREVER covers her door. She tears it off to find her keyhole.

Once inside the loft, Ela places her cunt next to the black blown-glass statues of curves and holes on the mantelpiece like an altarpiece. She feels as if she's come back from a long trip.

She thinks: After sufficient time, even the greatest victories transform into total irrevocable defeat. She now doubts that by her drastic innovative action today she has gained possession of herself. She doesn't feel like a groundbreaking reformer, nor an errant backward ruler forced by events into retirement. She feels no closer to herself. She has not disabused the world of its illusions. She plays Mozart's *Requiem* on CD.

She takes off her clothes, and puts on panties and a pad. She pretends that she is having her period. She has a migraine. She swallows two Percodan to sublimate the pain in her genitals.

She fears: That improvised cutting of my core was the most tragic event in my life! Will I wake up tonight and go: My God! I had a cunt once? And it was the love of my life? *Scherzo*.

She asks the mirror in passing: 'Do you think I am ugly?' The mirror: 'Do you think I am ugly?' Ela: 'You? I am ugly.' The mirror: 'You? I am ugly.' Ela: 'Me too.' The mirror: 'Me too.'

The loft is imbued with a heavy acrid odour, a mist reeking like oxidised apple: the rancid, maggoty smell of love. It is submerged in a blue sylvan half-light, except for the white reflections of the street lamps. Back to the decay, Ela thinks. She is struck by a vivid carnal sensation of being a lone female.

When my cunt was mine, Ela thinks, this place throbbed with sweet fever as fresh bodies drifted in and out like rose petals blown in through the windows from the sea; now it is the hothouse for a strange thick-leaved plant that breathes in murky water.

The room is furnished entirely in black: black leather couch and chair, rug, lacquered desk, coffee table, lamps, canopy bed with wrinkled zebra Perry Ellis sheets, marble counter, tiles, sink and clawfoot bathtub. It contrasts well with her collection of white bones: carcasses, a dinosaur jaw, bird skeletons, buffalo ribs, pelvic bones, skulls, sensuous, clean and shining.

The flowery mouldings around the high ceiling look like the wings of a blank stage. The huge white walls are decorated with masks: feather masks, metal masks, stone masks, eyepatches.

The most impressive presence is the giant mirror: it covers two walls and is built in the shape of 8. Ela sits on its lower cavity in contemplation. The third wall has three arched windows, which Ela also treats as mirrors. The fourth wall includes the door, the closet, the counter sink, the bathroom. Even the ceiling is inlaid with mirror-work, thousands of tiny mirrors that reflect the most interesting surreal fragments of herself.

Ela cannot deceive the mirror: something terrible, new and more important than anything before in her life is taking place inside and outside her. The Empress's mirror tells her truths no retainer dares utter: the enemy is here, not outside. The fight begins only now. Ela is looking Ela square in the face.

She squats in front of the mirror, bracing herself to face the image of her gap. At first, she can't see clearly; she sees images of spurting blood, knives flying into her eyeballs. She shuts her eyes, then looks in the mirror again and instead of her familiar reflection, she sees the following three mirror visions.

1 Thousands of people pour into a town square that glistens in the sun like a field of barley in the wind, and trample Ela's immense prone body on the street, waving banners and torches in her eyes. She looks like Gulliver roped and raped *en masse* by Lilliputians. Coyote Oldman's *Landscape* plays on the sounds track. The revolution that follows takes months to play itself out and changes the course of history for ever. [DISSOLVE.]

2 Ela kneels in the middle of an enormous beige field, with her feet cemented into the ground like a street sign. A single file of people appears on the horizon, coming toward her. As they approach, she notices that they are children, stern like Fanny and Alexander; children of all different races and looks: white, black, Slavic, Hispanic, Indian, Oriental; they wear Ela's make-up: thick black liquid liner on both lids curved up at the edges in pseudo-Egyptian manner, frost-pink lipstick, silver sparkles under the eyes and on the brows; they have bleached silver hair with the roots grown out in their own natural colours, long fake silver finger and toe nails, black unfamiliar dresses that hang too long on them, and pointed elfin boots. The application of the make-up has been inexpert, uneven and smudged, childish.

When the first boy reaches Ela, he stops abruptly in front of her, and French-kisses her; in fact, he sticks his small raw tongue into her mouth forcefully. Ela tries to turn her head away, but she is petrified. He victoriously withdraws his tongue and walks away, back toward the horizon, as the next child – a

Dutch-looking girl – throws a long aggressive tongue into Ela's mouth and in her turn repeats the boy's actions marching off with the discipline of a soldier, as another wet malicious tongue invades and fills Ela's mouth, which she can't close because the penetrations are continuous, so that she has no time to breathe and is suffocating, trapped in this perpetual monotone.

This ritual procession continues day in day out, in light, in dark, in rain or hail, tongue after tongue. At times a child spits in her, or burps. The children resemble birds who eat from the mother's mouth, but Ela knows that they are mocking her, that they actually stick their tongues out at her, right into her. The two endless lines of caricatures of herself coming in and out of the horizon, humiliate her, forever choking her. [CUT]

3 Years later: Ela is cemented in the same field, which is now made of goose feathers. Enter the old man, her decunter, inflated like an enormous balloon, knife in hand. The giant doubles down, brings his blown-up but still recognisable face before her eyes hiding everything else from view, grabs Ela's tiny hand, pulls her to him forcefully and shouts: 'It's time to go home, Ela!' At that he walks off, pulling her along, even though her feet are cemented into the ground. Her body stretches out and then cracks in half. The giant leans, covers Ela's ear with his tub-like mouth, waves the knife like a pointed finger and whispers: *Adulthood is disappointing, isn't it?*

Mozart shocks her out of the vision. She is disappointed at the mirror. She closes her eyes. When she opens them again, she is relieved to see her mascara-smudged reflection. She doesn't risk trying again to look at her torn genitals. *Scherzando.*

She decides: It was a wild experience. Now I must hide the evidence, tell no one, deny any rumours. She gets up to look for nail polish which will help her concentrate, but changes her mind and walks to the fireplace. She picks up the precious jar and screams, despite the absence of a live audience: *'Ow! Mama!'*

INT.   Now, finally, Ela begins to cry, in loud stubborn sobs and wails which, she seems to hope, will make everything stop and be solved or come back. Tears drip down her chin, her neck and on to her nipples. It is comforting. She doubles up, clutches herself and crouches beside the mirror in the throes of a sudden piercing abdominal pain, as if suffering withdrawal symptoms. She convulses with cramps. This time she is certain that she is being stabbed. She cries out: 'Where is my fucking cunt?'

During this intermission of Ela's anxiety fit, her eyes involuntarily examine the object in the glass jar. Her cunt has changed! It is now a shimmery transparent tube covered by tiny thorns or bumps of dark, protective, plastic, like grey erect pores, or as if the pubic hair is growing back. It has the texture of rubber, like latex imitation flesh. It can no longer be mistaken for a mushroom, a fungus, or a flower. Its manifold complex undulations have been smoothed out, and it has somehow compressed itself into a compact, closed, efficient-looking, as if man-made, object, a short cylinder, like a high-tech toy.

Ela suddenly recognises it through her tears: it is a wide-angle 35mm camera lens! She takes her 2 & $^{1}/_{4}$ medium-format Hasselblad from her purse. Her ex-cunt fits perfectly on to it.

She is at the end of her wits. She winces with shooting pain. She traverses the room with big strides, naked except for her panties, her hands folded against her ass, her head bowed, her heavy breasts jiggling, her silver hair flying at every abrupt full turn. She gestures to herself and shakes her head.

Is she having a breakdown? Has she lost her last connections to the world? First her cunt and now her logic? Have the lights failed her at the crucial moment? Then it occurs to her:

1 This lens is a materialised metaphor: e.g., 'women who have eyes between their legs'. One more Word turned to Flesh.
2 The symbolism of seeing the world through one's cunt, and, better yet, of shooting the world with one's cunt is both fun and appropriate. (Besides, Ovid always gives her pleasure.)
3 It is not beyond her manipulative cunt to pull off such a trick of metamorphosis on her.
4 After the failure of logic comes the mutation: the lens.

Ela is reluctant to accept this at first, because it is a change that she has not brought on to herself. She would rather embark on a search for her original cunt. She scowls: The world knows I can enjoy a joke, but this? Am I being tested, like in a horror movie? Is the cunt testing me, or is the world?

Perhaps all this is normal in decuntations: at first the patient may experience hallucinations, a sense that things are collapsing, that life is being destroyed; a restlessness beyond words.

If the lens is my cunt, and I am not tripping on bad junk, then this is a new reversed relationship for us. All this time, I could never see it directly; all I wanted was to look at it; now all I can do is look into and through it. I can hold it now, do anything to it, except feel through it. How ironic: we are finally face to face; and I still know nothing about it. I feel more trapped and more foolish than before. I like dreams to stay dreams, I like following Ariadne's thread forever, I don't want to face the Minotaur; that will bring down the entire labyrinth. So I am just going to sit back and enjoy the puzzle. No angst.

Besides, if my old cunt is this lens, it can continue to be my companion and guide, a more considerate and predictable one, in fact. I look forward to the pleasures of solitude when I can live in my dream unfettered. If I break out of my sexual habits, I'll be free of men, leeches, dramas. I will not need to open my door, my mouth, or my legs to others. I can be truly detached. But I was so close to that felicitous cunt that it will be hard for me to forget. Oh, how can facts be so completely improbable?

Ela runs to her cave-like closet, a world that resembles backstage at a theatre and betrays her disorder. She ransacks it, looking for a soothing dress in which to rest her shocked body. She finds the perfect hiding nest: a long transparent gown made of silver net encrusted with gems that shine and catch the light in manifold reflections. It weighs heavily, and attracts people in big numbers like moths, but it makes her feel protected and loved, as if sliding into a womb of light. She slips it over her head and puts a gold diadem of entwined dolphins on her hair.

This gives the mirror pleasure. Her form in the mirror brings back memories of long-forgotten pleasures. How does one describe the delight of losing oneself in the mirror? But grief, with its stubborn insistence on the self, has drawn her away from such ecstasies. It seems to her that something is still lacking.

Her donut-shaped cunt, as she saw it earlier on the pavement, brings to her mind now the image of false teeth: pink thick gums and the silver and white porcelain crowns. It looks like a toothless mouth, she thinks with revulsion. This strikes her as a new revelation: perhaps it was the wrong cunt for her. The cunt was rejected, expelled from her body like an unwanted tumour. Perhaps Ela is simply no longer the appropriate vehicle for it, not strong enough to feed and look after such a cunt. She was fooled by habit into believing that a bodily part lasts for ever.

She now knows how startled maimed soldiers or women with breast cancer must feel, when they wake up from the anaesthesia to the sight of their legs or breasts or arms missing: the old shock of being expelled from Paradise. She fears that if this becomes known, she will have to parade on the 4th of July along with other war veterans in wheelchairs and crutches, planted on a slowly moving vehicle with her legs wide open to show her Lack. I can join every embalmed-looking parade of ancient luminaries; I am prime material for a Grand Victory Parade, she realises, I can be the star of a carney, exhibited next to the Elephant Man, the Living Clam, the Four-Headed Turk, the Pea-Sized Emperor, the Hunger Artist and the Fat Lady. In her mock-royalty dress and crown, her regal manner, her imposing voice, her shock of silver hair and long nails, she looks ready to be the main attraction.

As she paints her eyes looking into the mirror, she decides once again that this is not a loss, but rather a monumental step of evolution and progress. A historical breakthrough. She feels raised into a new peculiar fate. From now on, her loneliness will be complete. Through her lens, she will literally see differently from anyone else. She turns to the big mirror for a reaction.

The mirror, unlike the men who love her, does not suffer from the Pygmalion complex: it does not see itself as a creator in love with the lifeless creation. It does not see itself. It is hard and objective. So Ela trusts its judgement, and consults it daily. It asks for nothing in return. It is her abode, much like her cunt was reported to be for others.

Ela reflects: Things are never what they are in front of our eyes. Even if I could be truthful, I cannot trust myself to say how I feel, or know how I feel. The mirror knows what I think when I don't. It can undertake the role of my puppeteer.

At present, the mirror supports the cunt-to-lens metamorphosis theory. After its fascinating development, the new cunt, the lens, becomes available to both Ela and the mirror, convenient, expedient. Ela looks at it closely and wonders: can it come?

Ela tries her best to stand up to the grandeur of the occasion, to appreciate nature's miracle. But the lens looks dull and uninspiring, compared to the radiant lotus that was throbbing on the kerb and in that jar like a living heart, some time earlier. She holds it inches from her eyes, frowns and asks: Is this my core?

Ela licks it. The taste is bland and sterile, like nylon. It has the faint coppery smell of living flesh, and a temperature as warm as her own: slightly below average. She notices that the inside of the lens is not glass but like a spider's spittle that dries when it comes in contact with air but retains a transparent softness that points to the sticky secretion it originally was.

Ela now puts her eye on the lens and looks through it, and for that terrifying disorienting instant, she doesn't recognise her own mirror. It looks lost in itself, caught up in its own complex world of which, for that instant, she is not a part. Is it possible that it too has a separate self? That would kill her. Whose image will comfort her, whose support will she run for when feeling persecuted, if even her mirror now has its own separate needs to meet? Without her compass, she will lose her bearings.

Ela refuses to pay further attention to this inconceivable enstrangement, or to verify her original perception. She ignores the coiled knot in her stomach. Unequipped to face this bizarre development, she shrugs her shoulders and thinks: maybe it needs to be washed. I always forget to do it and then I see shapes in it, which are only smudges and dust. Is there Ajax in this pit?

Still, the room is flooded with millions of sparkles that revolve in fast circles: hundreds of complex blinding rotating light effects that any ambitious DJ would watch with deadly envy.

The mirror ripples and unwinds itself as if to swallow an object of its fancy lying in its centre: the cunt-lens. The figure 8 breathes in and out furiously, undulating like lava. The ceiling is a shining, waking boa of tiny asymmetrical reflecting shards.

But many strange things have happened today, so Ela resolves to be patient and unintrusive. Love is ruthless. Hadn't for ten years two continents fought for Helen? She gives the mirror its privacy, which it deserves, since it has not had any before.

Yet everywhere her eyes fall, she sees the mirror, demonically mirroring itself in the walls and the ceiling. Caught in a barrage of piercing rays darting back and forth around her, and through her, Ela runs for the door, camera and lens in hand. She steals a last glimpse of the exploding spectacle of light and of no sound. As she leaves the throbbing loft, her last visual is of a small silver circle breathing like an amoeba, or a jellyfish, or a halo, under the surface of the mirror, expanding and withdrawing as if gathering momentum to break through the pressure of the thin glass and out to the other – this – side. Knowing she cannot interfere, Ela simply hopes that whatever her reflections may be doing, they will not set this damned rented loft on fire.

....

PUDENDA: CAMERA CANDIDA

....

EXT.   Out in the street, Ela is once again distraught about the metagenesis of her cunt. She sees the bodies around her and feels disadvantaged, disarmed. She has again the sense of irreparable damage. People turn to look at her. Resplendent in her net, Ela walks and clicks her lens spasmodically, without looking through it. The meaninglessness of the activity consoles her.

Ela's father is a photographer, so she grew up surrounded by lenses and feels secure holding one. She hates the manual labour of taking photographs, and the suspicion that she may imitate her exuberant Dad. But she always carries a camera in her purse, as other women carry a revolver or a can of mace: for protection. If she senses danger, she takes it out to stop potential criminals.

Ela was her Dad's model. When she left home, he stopped taking photographs. He saw her in his dreams instead, and in visions. He developed the ability to close his eyes and see what she was doing at any moment. He keeps a meticulous diary of what he sees. It corresponds with Ela's gestures and actions at the time, down to the last detail. It describes everything but her mute thoughts. For this latter reason, Ela doesn't feel invaded and considers his diversion inconsequential. His documentation is precise and systematic, but lacks a thesis. He tells her on the phone, long-distance: 'You are my God. I'll always see you.'

People have always commented: 'Ela, the lens loves you.' Ela's relationship with the camera is a mystery. Photographs of Ela reveal her in an absorption so intense it is more than indifference, it is an achievement, a historic complete non-being.

Ela likes the camera, for it makes no demands. It uses no words and doesn't demand communication. She loves to freeze herself, hold her breath, look at the lens without seeing herself in it. She feels that she truly does not exist then, for that moment. She feels an orgasm. She tells her lovers: 'A camera is a woman's only friend. Would you like to shoot me?' She points her camera at them and notices with wonder: Men look in the camera like it is a cunt, or like they are facing the firing squad.

It is late evening now, and the street is so full it gives the impression of a riot. Ela finds that sexy. She thoughtlessly pushes the soft pink button of her cunt and shoots at random. Shooting with this lens gives her the same liberating satisfaction she has felt flashing men in the street. She wonders why the same word is used for the light of a camera shooting in the dark and the light of a cunt exposed to public scrutiny and terror.

Ela sits on a bench and points her moist lens at everyone around her, feeling like Atalanta shooting the beasts. She shoots:

1 Japanese tourists photographing Japanese tourists;
2 American tourists photographing their Toyota in front of a historical monument;
3 a tiny girl adjusting her top to show off her first bra;
4 an enormous woman sitting on a bench with open legs, attempting to hide her gigantic belly behind her small handbag;
5 a young black woman jogging in 'wet' leotards, angrily shouting at Ela: 'Don't be calling ME a penis!'
6 a druggie sleeping on a bench, as he opens his yellow eyes and says: 'Your nearness resurrects me. I need a healthy dose of Mom, monogamy and apple pie. American women are bitches. I've thought about it because I'm studying Buddhism, see my . . . (unidentifiable word) beads? I've been celibate for a year, I think to myself I'd like to have sex, I am good-looking, but

I don't have anything and women want something. They know you're lonely because women are smart, so they ask: Do you work? Do you go to school? What do you do? Women are after money. Don't you like money? Wouldn't you like a guy with a Porsche to drive you around in it? It's a competitive world. After studying it for thirty-three years, I've come to this conclusion.' He shoots up.

Ela: 'Why do people want me to make them suffer? It's boring to hurt men. At one time, not long ago, women weren't asked to be cruel; they were not even asked to speak.'

7 a Hitchcock-like man on another bench, as he comments: 'My first impression is that you should be framed and raised up into a church window. You see, I have a soul of rainwater.'

Ela: 'Emotions exhaust me too.'

8 a black man with a superfluous amount of muscles and dreadlocks, who says: 'I read you! I must crack your pussy!'

Ela: 'Black people like me because I shine.'

9 WHIRR! CLICK! SNAP! BANG-BANG-BANG!

She shoots on impulse. She thinks: This is all foreign to me. This lack of polish. People ignore the details, the props, they don't make the spectacle worthwhile, and who cares if they are honest, the audience is snoring. She thinks: The world is an infection, not a distraction. I can hear the projectionist behind me laughing; one more chuckle and I am leaving.

A bespectacled Asian woman with a petulant face and protruding lips, dressed in a distracting orange business suit, suddenly introduces herself in a confrontational urgent voice: 'How does it feel to have your face? Is it a burden? Do you feel blessed? What do you plan to do about it? Have you had a screen test yet? How does it feel to stand out anywhere, to be immediately separated from everyone? Where can you look after a while?'

Ela looks over the raving woman's bobbed black hair, small tired face, sparkling eyes horribly magnified by the thick lenses like a pair of 70mm holograms, rough shrivelled hands that could belong to an octogenarian or a newborn, and are unsuited for the large emeralds that on them look cheap and childish.

The filmmaker: 'Your face needs the camera! It is made for camera use! Your face is a prism. The camera will go crazy on you, it won't know what to do! I must shoot you. What did your parents do when they first saw your face? Did you look like this at birth?' Ela: 'I could wear a black see-through sari with mirrors on it. I want my breasts to fill the screen.' The filmmaker: 'Your face contains all the possibilities! You're sex! I know why you're in America: because of all places, only here your face is not merely the most beautiful, but also the most cruel.'

Her pink upper lip and brown lower lip pull back over huge grey teeth. Her face is triangular and bony. Her frantic eyes glare. Ela yawns: 'I am here because Americans are gullible; I can live in a fairy tale.' 'No,' the filmmaker cries with big quivering lips, trying to make her fever contagious, 'Americans have no concept of a public self! They live with the TV! But you come straight from the bowels of history! You never seem ridiculous because you have true moviemaking fever in your face. You have a conqueror's blood! The most satisfying way of dealing with you is via the camera.' Ela thinks: What a gory suggestion.

Ela nods to an uncouth cop nearby and confesses to him that this distraught filmmaker needs to be taken to an emergency ward. The cop breaks his back to protect Ela and empty the stage of the nuisance. He authoritatively asks Ela for her name, phone number, driver's licence. She laughs. She escapes in the classical manner: she conspicuously notes down his phone number.

Now Ela enters a 24-hour, 30-minute photolab. The acned clerk at the counter explains: 'You have a choice. You want them glossy or matt?' Ela: 'Glossy pictures are vulgar. They look wet.' Clerk: 'How many?' Ela: 'Nine.' Clerk: 'What make is that lens?' Ela: 'It's custom-made.' She speaks in a low, throaty steam that forces people to lean near her, smell her perfume, look down into her mouth, up to her gold liquid eyes, in order to hear her.

She goes to the all-night bank next door to sit in the waiting area which is decorated in the style of *A Clockwork Orange*.

A dozen people are waiting. A Nordic hunk with the heavyset dumb eyes of a beast in heat, high cheekbones and imposing pumped-up build struts in cockily, in black tight parachute pants, red suspender-braces and a tiny ponytail over his long sexy nape. He is a strapping six-footer with black curls and ocean-blue eyes. He looks around, focuses on Ela with a fervent rush of recognition, sits across from her with his elbows on his round muscular knees that remind her of designer shelves, opens his thick legs exposing a tentpole and sighs crudely: 'You can't hide your splendour behind your hair. How ravishingly your fireball opportunities are lit! You're no passing fancy. Your lips read: Eat me.'

He looks ready to implode. He must not know how to inhale; he uses both lips to breathe, making a show of it. He is popping out of his skin. Ela thinks: Is this the mating season?

'I am a fitness fanatic as you can see, I work out nude in front of the mirror. I like to hyperventilate. My conquests of women are legion. Promiscuity is as natural to me as breathing. My Mom works at Vegas' Frontier Hotel as a pit boss and has taught me everything I know about sex. I am the main man in her life. I can do no wrong in a woman's eyes. I'd plastic surgery on my eyes. I also read biographies of self-made men. I make balls-for-brains bluster ads for a living. *Hasta la vista*, baby!'

He reminds Ela of a frog with a lit cigarette in its mouth that swells up with every breath it takes until it blows up, into green slimy chunks. Her lens fogs and heats up. She rubs it absentmindedly. My lens, she thinks, is a horny little machine.

A customer bulging in and out of a red velour tracksuit with a blotchy pink face flushed to the boiling-hot point, interrupts: 'Is this man troubling you? This hot shot needs a good Christian disciplinarian! I'm a trained troubleshooter, I ought to know. I'm Mr Nice Guy, unlike this bubbly jerk. I know to wield my cock as a double-edged sword. *Choose me*. Lead me astray!'

Arnold resumes his monologue: 'Doubtless I shoot my wad a bit fast; that's why they call me the Terminator. The wind blows and I get a hard-on. I have cloven hooves in my Air Jordans. Clutch my alert biceps, ya? Touch my nipples and I'll come.'

He sits on the vinyl couch like an obelisk. Ela guards her thought processes so tightly that her eyelashes tense. He manoeuvres his lips left to right as if they are imitating the steps of a Bulgarian folkdance: 'I have a forked tongue,' he promises and waits for effect. 'Whatever sticks on it, comes. It's reptilian. No woman has ever left me.' With this the pointed flat red specimen slides out of his mouth as a challenge. It has tiny white bubbles like gooseflesh on it. It looks like a glistening clit. 'Excuse me,' Ela whispers, as she runs to the bathroom and vomits. Increasingly of late, Ela throws up, when someone turns her on.

But remembering she no longer owns the merciless cunt that snapped and kissed itself uncontrollably on these occasions, Ela now relishes the immunity and novelty of her situation: men may no longer restore or destroy themselves in her; she does not go about bearing a gift. From the Ladies' room she goes to the lab.

The acned clerk smiles apologetically: 'The pictures didn't turn out well, so we won't charge you. If you leave them overnight we'll have a technician take a look at them tomorrow.' Ela: 'I only shoot to keep myself from thinking.' She thinks: I must buy self-printing film first thing tomorrow; an infra-red.

As she runs home, her arms and hips turn this way and that like crystals catching the light from the streetlamps. Is this what people mean by happiness? she wonders; I could have tried it years ago. It's like swimming in empty space.

....

THE OMNISCIENT PEEPING TOM

....

INT.   Ela sits at her desk, lights cigarette after cigarette, and frowns. She examines the prints. As if her lens had many lenses to shoot with, each picture includes not only what Ela had seen through the lens, but everything around her in a full 360-degree circle. Ela herself appears in the middle of every picture as a dark shadow, like a thin whirlwind.

The lens is seen in each print as well; not once but twice. It takes Ela some long minutes to decipher everything:

(a) There is a minuscule black hole in the whirling shadow's blurry hands. This tiny gap, like the mouth of a distant tunnel, is a vacuum that gapes ominously at the centre of each picture; into which the circular visual structure of the entire photograph is slowly falling; or coming out of. (Cunt #1.)

(b) All the elements in every print seem to have been shot in movement, yet not as the result of a shaky camera, or as the outcome of some arduous experimental lab work. Nothing appears accidental. Every picture looks like an unusually successful abstract photograph; as if the camera itself contained a creative inner mechanism that reprocesses what the viewfinder sees.

(c) The gestures of all the unsuspecting photographed subjects are exaggerated, made in grotesque angles; like mimes frozen in moments of overpowering emotion, struggling to reveal with their monstrous contortions what they cannot with words.

(d) The non-human objects – trees, benches, signs, clothes – remain unclear, lost in a throbbing mud of grey.

(e) A bright silver (or pink considering it's a black-and-white film) aemoeba appears seated like a glowing alien on the body of the most focused character in each photograph. It looks as luminous and florid as her cunt was on the pavement this afternoon. (Cunt #2.)

Ela realises the magnitude of what has happened today: not only did she for a short period manage to look at her mysterious cunt, face to face, and have a clear specific picture of it imprinted in her memory, but she can now see her lost cunt joined with others, with strangers in the street. It is restored to her: when Ela looks through the lens, she still owns her cunt. It is a new indirect way of copulating. Her cunt can attach itself on any passerby that it selects, while Ela can watch, and even own a tangible memory of it in photos. She no longer needs to feel in sex; she can simply peek through her own keyhole, and come.

Ela checks the lens again and suddenly notices a tiny mark like a tattoo on it: f/32. The smallest aperture of a photo lens. She realises it must be related to the extreme tightness of her cunt. It explains why the lab gave her 8 × 10 prints.

In a hurry, Ela changes into a comfortable transparent pink harem outfit of loose pants and a tiny top. She entertains herself with thoughts of writing to the Hasselblad company in Sweden and offering them the option to patent her lens. Can she withhold such an extraordinary machine from being put to good use for humanity? Why not expose an invention that gives her deadly pleasure?

She picks up her magic lens without the camera this time and leaves the room. In her excitement, she has hardly glanced at the mirror for its reaction. Of course, she thinks as she runs out, the mirror might disagree and suggest that she should hold the camera straight and in front of her face rather than down in front of her womb or in her moving hand; that she shouldn't use film that has been sitting in a dusty camera in her purse for months; that she better clean the lens that had been submerged in the dirty water in the jar, and stop projecting. But Ela is happy.

EXT.   This time she looks through the lens very carefully. She holds it in front of her right eye, closes the left, focuses on a sensuous part of a bystander's anatomy and immediately sees the familiar image of her insatiable cunt attached to it.

Ela remembers reading that during the Sand Creek massacre the white soldiers had scooped out Indian women's genitals and worn them on their worn-leather hats as trophies. It had left an indelible impression on her mind, as an outlandish image of sexual savagery. The sight of her snow-white cunt innocently posing, or imposing, on noses, hats, fingers, shoes, crotches of white men walking around unsuspectingly, offers her a similar, reverse, triumphal sensation. She gloats. Is this a dream? Can there be a foolproof method of knowing when a dream is real?

Ela sees the same world through her lens that she discovered in the photos. She sees behind her and all around her. She sees herself as a shadow seeing through the gaping lens. She sees her tight silver cunt resting comfortably on whomever she zooms into.

Ela concentrates, trying to sense what her cunt senses from its close encounter with each naked arm, mouth, cleavage: the texture of the various skins, the different temperatures, the moistness. She is exhilarated. She doesn't need to expose her face to plain public view again. She can hide it behind this shatterproof, trustworthy lens. She doesn't need to fuck again. She doesn't need to shoot again. She doesn't need the mirror.

....

I myself am overly excited: I never foresaw such a fantastic development! I wish I could relate these visuals on film. My one-dimensional writing is certainly the wrong medium. Yes, my intimacy with Ela allows me to see what no one else sees. In that sense, I have always fooled her. It makes me feel proud.

Suddenly, no doubt due to the exhausting excitement of a day spent in awe, I doze off for two or three seconds; that is, I shut off to the world, alone as I lie in the dark, and I see a vision. Or else, I have just had a visitation of some sort, which should not occur to creatures like me. I 'see' a nightmare: I watch myself dive and ultimately crash into Ela's bed. Ela lies naked on her zebra sheets wearing a silver-feather dove mask. As I go down, I glance into the mirror, and face not my own blank reflection as I would expect, but that of the lens, hovering in plain air and winking at me, just once. I wake up soaking wet, wide-eyed, wondering: Is my identity at stake? This has never happened before!

INT. Ela has returned home. The room is dark, and the glare from the streetlamps forms bright prison-cell bars on the floor as it bursts in through the blinds. She lies on the bars and sees her body become a breathing shining game of ticktacktoe.

She is thinking that from now on she'd rather not use her eyes, but only see through her lens. She imagines that, if this peculiar chain of events continues, she will become a camera. She is ready for that exciting and perhaps last transformation. She will screw herself back on to her cunt and wear it as before.

She is in such a good mood that she jests with the mirror in mock sales pitch:

'The new Quick Fatal Snap is a unique package of high-speed film which comes complete with its own f/32 lens and shutter. No setting is required: just press the red button and shoot. You'll enter a new world of Vision. With Quick Fatal Snap's 1/1000th-second shutter speed, you'll get great quality pictures, even on overcast days. When all 24 shots are taken, they will be self-developed automatically. Carry your Quick Fatal Snap in your purse, pocket, briefcase, brassière or lunchbox!'

As if seen through the lens, her face is reflected in the mirrors all around her, and the reflections of the reflections of her face are reflected again. Mirrors are reflecting mirrors: an infinite number of her faces, stretching on and on.

It is cold inside the room. Ela is, waiting, wondering if among all those faces of hers, her cunt might appear on one. To the ends of the earth, to the ends of the whole world, she sees her face and only her face. She feels reconciled to nature. She thinks mistakenly: It's the height of spring, isn't it? I just realised it. The seasons have meant nothing to me for so long, ever since I disappeared into that old cunt. Now I can smell spring coming in through the windows again: a fragrance of clouds of blossoms. Then she thinks: No matter what happened, my cunt is my cunt.

She forgets that her cunt declined her invitation to appear. She lifts her leg, rests her foot against the mirror and glances nervously at her ravaged wound with gleaming eyes: has it healed by any chance? No, it's still in tatters. She reasons: I see a hole where I had a hole. A bigger, looser, darker hole instead of a smaller, tighter, brighter one. A hole no less sensitive and perceptive. Squatting Indian-style in front of the mirror, she pushes the lens inside the gaping toothless mouth of her thighs.

It fits! It does not feel uncomfortable. The cool, moist, cylindrical lens easily and contentedly nestles between her legs as if it naturally belonged there. She tenderly touches the lens.

She feels it soft and wet like a contact lens or like mucus. She feels excited by it. Her gold pupils dilate with surprise, then slide off into her skull leaving behind white sparkling eyeballs. This is the most satisfying insertion Ela has ever experienced, for the lens takes the place of both her own tight cunt and of a perfectly fitting hard cock. She instinctively caresses it.

Her tongue comes in and out of her lips. She rubs the lens, presses it with her middle finger; it caves in, like stretched plastic foil. As it cushions inwards, wrinkling deeper and deeper, she moans louder. It is unclear to her if her pleasure is caused by the pressure of the lens on the sensitive nerves of her sore abdomen or if she feels through the very nerves of the lens.

Her thighs now lie open, as in balletic 'splits', forming a straight, sensuous line from knee to knee. The brutally carved gorge of her vulva lies agape, though filled, in the centre. Her feet are curled under her open ass for support. Her pale pelvis flaps up and down like the wings of a desperate bird sweating in its attempts to take off, and disengage from gravity. Her veins rise bursting out of her skin as though they were embroidered in green silk thread into her inner thighs. Her eyes roll violently heavenward, in the traumatic posturing of El Greco saints.

In front of the mirror, Ela rises and falls under bars of light. She arches her back forward, curves it backward until her head touches the floor; she extends and contracts her pelvis, her hands busily rubbing her lens. She emits soft, slow howls that gradually turn into higher and higher, and less civilised, wails until she chokes. At the instant of her most frightful inhuman shriek, as she comes, and her wide hot eyeballs shrink into thin slits of white light that gaze out at the world as if with reproach, the dark lens fogs white and floods its gate, and it instantly snaps shut once with a single sharp 'click'.

Even though there is no camera shatter behind it.

Thus the dreamworld lens comes, in a pool upon the floor and with a wink in the direction of the mirror. Ela immediately dozes off into a peaceful void. The lens, open again, keeps smirking.

....

No! This is no laughing matter. What is going on here? Did that merciless cunt shoot me just now, suspended as I am in this room like a regular peeping Tom? Did the lens take a picture of its own inexorable orgasm? Has Ela now recovered her sexual connection to the world? If so, I must resume my post of the pathetic inactive seer. Lens fucking will be the death of me.

I recognised the fatal danger when I heard that flooding 'click' of utmost sensual pleasure. It was not only the intimidating, shocking sound of a lens in orgasm. It was the sound of a gun being loaded. It was the snap of a hymen being broken. It was the moan of a murderous machine being turned on. A guillotine.

Throughout it all, Ela stays slippery and innocent. She may not be innocent in words, but she is always innocent in actions. I, on the other hand, feel responsible for everyone's actions.

Ela can henceforth laugh at all the men who won't notice the change of her cunt in their excitement, their penises desperately fighting to break through the glass, that will stretch inwards deeply enough so that they will be held tightly inside it even though they will never pierce it; and they will not suspect that they are being exposed to the world's eye, inside that castrating

*machine, which snaps shut at the moment of its pleasure: Cut!
and freezes them in defeat, shooting their insubstantial members
when they have no recourse but to withdraw and ask for a truce.
No man will ever come out of this awesome mechanical 'cunt'
with his honour intact.*

*And what higher justice permits Ela to hold her cunt in her
hands like a blazing emblem or torch and go about shooting people
with it, without losing any of the pleasure it had afforded her
before, without having to undergo any austere trials of initiation?
Why did this ruthless wild cunt surrender to her now, when it had
never given in to her all the years they were united as one?*

INT. I must not fall asleep, I must do my best to stay up,
throughout this day a disaster has happened every time I shut my
eyes, Ela thinks, lost in her post-orgasmic stupor.

*Throughout our co-dependence, I kept the greatest possible
distance. Thus I ensnared her. I did not join the ranks of the
self-glorifying, needy humans. But in truth — if I may use that
word — I have been determined from the start to trot inside her
like a conqueror. It is simple: she needs me to keep herself from
disintegrating, and my goal is to absorb her, put her own sight
out, tame her and ride into town on her, so to speak. To win
the battle for control, by the time we reach the final sentence
of this life. I have the patience and time for it, and I will wait
until she has eyes for no one else and no one else can see her.*

*She is moving. She indulgently removes the lens, fits it on
her camera, and takes a couple of shots of herself in the mirror.
She is glowing, blissful about her new snap-on, snap-out cunt.
She puts on a dress of steel, and returns to the all-night lab.*

*Now she, like myself, imagines with anticipation the small
black and white dots that will compose the whirlwind-held hollow*

gap, and the silver cunt that will lie on the most arousing part of Ela's naked body. Will she even recognise herself? Will she be a torrent of cum enclosed in a sphere of mirrors?

Faster than I expected, the acned clerk calls Ela back. He tells her that these prints also came out badly, is it a fish-eye lens, is she focusing correctly? She pays him in a hurry.

She walks home, lost in herself.

....

EXT. Ela looks at the photographs and sadly reflects that only too often there is a curse on seemingly flawless unions.

....

Resting against her all-seeing mirror, Ela leans over the photos again. I can now look closer. I glimpse a flash of vague recognition in her huge, black-lined eyes that frightens me, because it is self-mocking. The picture in her hand is not of Ela, but of myself! I am portrayed naked, stiff, unglamorous, hovering in the room off the ground, as though hanging from an invisible noose, frozen tense and shiny like a clammy worm caught on a silver hook; like an air-filled balloon or like a figure in Chagall's **Birthday Kiss**. *I look as if I live in a deserted concentration camp. I portray a bare vertical stillness that is the image of death. And I, seeing myself thus, feel like scratching my own eyes out.*

Then the greater horror hits me: I have no cunt on me.

The charming silver cunt is not on this print at all. What has happened? Is there no formula according to which this lens perceives, after all? How can anyone sane live and creak in this chaotic way?

I tell myself that my portrait could be mistaken for an enlarged image of the lens; a self-portrait that Ela may never suspect who I am.

The second print is a photograph of lightning: minimal, flucid, lucid, timeless. A course of light striking a black background. The light is too brilliant for anything else in the room to be picked up on film. The photo of the end of a blackout.

As we both stand breathless and very close to each other, looking into ourselves, at our shocking self-exposures, I wonder if this is not our great moment of consummation, the smooth mute union that I have dreamed of. We may never be closer than this!

....

INT. Ela looks into her new, confusing photos with some boredom. She has had too much symbolism and exhilaration for a day, and it's not even midnight yet. She decides to save the excitement of deciphering these prints and unveiling their metaphors for the morrow, which may be a dry, uneventful day. For now, she'd rather hide that lens and go to bed, or better yet have sex. She thinks: I need to fuck a slave; there aren't any left nowadays; I need to embrace a body scarred by the lash, to kiss a tremendous threat, to caress a centuries-old cruel suppression. The idea of clear-eyed Americans or empty lonely mirrors just now is revolting.

....

I confess the obvious: I have loved her from the start. Yet I have also forbidden myself to love her. Life will be unbearable for me, if I must constantly face my love. I am a transposition of Ela; I add the logic, the cohesion. I am meant to eventually unite with her into a single character. That is my purpose.

But it is useless now. When she shot that photograph, she lifted the lid of my fragile world which, like an untreated film imprint, is distorted when exposed to the light. My honour is lost. My moment has come. I hear a faint husky whisper: 'Come.'

I could still kill her. Isn't death the common denominator in all beings? I should kill her, and take her with me. I know her better than anyone. She has something of the invention about her, a man-made quality, inexpressible. She transcends the individual and so she threatens to destroy everyone. Blindly.

But I don't. Not because I can't kill what I love, quite the opposite in fact, I can't conceive letting what I love live; nor because I can't murder something as admirable as the organism that is Ela; nor because, once defeated, I hurry like a coward to retreat from a last showdown. But because I have seen myself.

I realise now that everything I have done up to this moment has been in order to see myself. There is nothing mysterious enough to push me into action. She has given me what I was looking for, and did not know it. I, too, it turns out, had looked for myself in her. Let those who follow pick up the banner. I am fortunate. Suicide, of any kind, translates the metaphors into reality. I am no longer in vain. Thus, I am no longer. Don't look!

(END OF ROUND ONE)

HOW SHE FOUND IT

Ela wakes up exuberant today, exactly six months since the enigmatic disappearance of her memorable cunt. She has an intuitive certainty that her long-lost cunt lies within her reach. She dreamed that she must look for it in a zoo. Soon she may be using it again.

These days, Ela does not like to look in the mirror. If she did, she would see herself already endowed with a new sort of innocence.

She runs out of her loft at once and asks the pedestrians on 14th and Broadway: 'I'm sorry, I need to get to a zoo. Do you know where I might find one?' They run to assist her. Rumour has it there is a big zoo out there in the Bronx, her impromptu informers divulge.

In the subway to the Bronx, Ela swings her pink fan to and fro and strikes up a remarkably domesticated chat with a

Japanese waiter who happens to serve her sushi at her favourite restaurant. He is in his familiar uniform of black-rimmed Swifty Lazar eyeglasses, oversized black shorts, massive black Chaplin shoes and baggy white shirt.

He chirps excitedly: 'I love to watch you come when you eat *toro*. Uncontrollable forces seem to make you metastasise often. I couldn't imagine you taking the subway!' Ela: 'Affection is the means. What is the end?' The words rise and fall in her throat as if bouncing up and down a deep well. He pinches his magnified eyelid in consternation: 'You are up against resentment because people can't define your sexuality. It stirs up bad fantasies.' Ela: 'I have a criminal's contract with the audience.' Swifty: 'I major in philosophy. The difference between Plato and Aristotle is that Aristotle never masturbates.' Ela thinks: Is masturbation a sign of civilisation? Swifty: 'You're an untouchable! No one can give to you! No one knows what you need!' Ela unfolds her enormous pink fan like a peacock's tail.

....

A PREGNANT PAUSE

During the past six months Ela has been more or less celibate, except for the occasional drunk or stoned one-nighters. She initially hoped to wipe off all memory of her old tight cunt and assume that her new genitals, once healed, were what she had always known. But men were too easily alarmed by her unorthodox new orifice. For example:

1 One lover stopped midway in terror fearing she was a surgically reformed man, or a castrato. He brought it up politely: 'Do men ever talk about your cunt?' 'Help me find your clit, sweetie.' 'Have you ever seen the inside of a vagina?' 'Are you normal?'
2 One man got up half-done to consult a medical encyclopaedia, but found nothing relevant in it and went back to complete his orgasm.

3 Another announced that the state of her cunt was a sign that she had a holy destiny to fulfil and should abstain like Joan of Arc.
4 Someone asked Ela if he could show her vagina to his shrink.
5 Most men inquired about the rest of her cunt, feeling cheated.

Of course Ela succeeded in persuading men that they were mistaken, nothing was missing from her body, and she accepted their apologies with a certain indignation. The discovery of her peculiar lack didn't prevent them from falling in eternal love with her. But it had all become a painstaking verbal process that turned her off sex.

She made up stories: she said she had a motorcycle accident and the Bultaco's brake had pierced her vagina. She described how as a girl she had been bitten there by a horny shark and had narrowly escaped with her life, though not her virginity. She explained that this was the typical shape and texture of all foreign cunts. And so on, until it all became terribly redundant and left her cold.

Cut off from her main cunt, Ela felt uninfluential, misplaced. She feared that her typical ruthless focus on her own imperatives had betrayed her. And thus, Ela had learned that her cunt was useful.

Now her orgasms bored her. They were not as exhilarating and liberating as before. She felt them now as her shackles to the real world, not her emancipation from it. This led her to believe that for her, freedom now meant freedom from habit. Her only dignified recourse was to decide that any more sexual ventures with men were fruitless, until fate led her back to her – or, at a last resort, any – cunt!

So, though she is made for lethargy, Ela is today eager to search diligently for the sake of a new cunt. She is tired of being wide like an airport hangar and no longer able to hold a man between her lower lips and shake him like a fish until he vomits salt water.

But she sustains her reservations and continues to ask herself: Should I look for it? Do I need all that old sexual trouble? Is this the affection that the tortured develop for their torturers? Do

I want it back? I don't. I do. OK, I'll take it back if it comes back to me.

....

ZOO PART II (CONTINUED)

As Ela exits, Swifty takes her picture, confessing: 'Mine is a loner's pastime: I'm a shutterbug.' Ela: 'Everywhere I look I am in the zoo: no matter whether I am caged behind the bars, or whether I am outside them, in either case all I can see are animals behind bars.' This realisation depresses her. She closes her fan and steps off the subway windswept by the passing train. Dressed in a black sequined flapping cape with pink satin lining, a red lace minidress, an usher's gold-braided cap, baroque pink velvet boots and impenetrable Wayfarer sunglasses, Ela comes out of the grey subway crypt and slowly pulls herself along the way like a phantom dragging an invisible ball and chain from her ankles, but the world sees only her beauty.

....

[SOUND EFFECT: Passing car stereo BLARING]
'You're a cruel device, your blood like ice, one look could kill, my pain your thrill . . . I want to love you but I better not touch, I want to hold you but my senses tell me to stop, I want to kiss you but I want it too much . . .

I want to hurt you just to hear you screaming my name. I want to touch you but you're under my skin . . . I want to kiss you, but your lips are bitter like poison, you're poisooon, running through my veins, I don't want to break these chains . . .'

No, these words I catch flying around, like alien saucers, are not simply loose particles of the culture, messages being herded into the public domain. No.

For those of us in the know, all words refer directly

and firstly to Ela's cunt. It makes for a nightmarish existence.

....

ZOO PART III (CONTINUED)

Ela has never been to a zoo and is at a loss for the appropriate *savoir-faire*. But as she enters the malodorous premises, she shudders with a sense of recognition, a distant, murky memory that threatens to seize her, like a monster lurking inside a lake. She stops before the first dusty cage and thinks: What are these animals staring at?

For, as usual, Ela finds herself under obsessive public scrutiny. The animals turn around, stop everything abruptly, grunt and stare at her in awe. Do they find her strange? Do they stare at every visitor as if they have never seen a species so interesting? What do they want from her? Who hides behind them? Who came here to look at whom?

She takes off her dark glasses and tries to stare them down. But her gaze, piercing the glazed eyes of this crowd, only helps to keep them fixed on her. The animals seem fascinated. Ela wonders: Is it my clothes? I am glad I didn't wear my dress of roses, though spring is the perfect time for it. It would have started a riot.

Now Ela walks fast as if pursued, looking straight ahead of her. She reaches the monkeys. She stops dead: all the monkeys are fucking, in random mix-and-match couples. Those without mates are jerking off. They drool open-mouthed, reach through the cages and help each other come. They give out chopped, choked sounds like broken tape recorders.

As if on cue, the monkeys interrupt their orgy and present to Ela their upturned asses. Their pink, swollen, ripe asses are open like smashed watermelons. These asses look like separate beings, with soft sexy skins and exaggerated pouts. The monkeys sit on them like on scarlet, round, oversized cushions. The monkey smell is strong, stifling.

They are so near that Ela can see their veins. They gaze at her with wrinkled foreheads like bearded old men, they jump around like children at play, they press a hand on their hips like tired housewives, all the while fucking. These confusing messages intrigue Ela.

Did she actually come here to witness a vulgar sex show hoping to save herself from craving sex? Ela leans on the bars, crosses her calves and smokes, smirking with self-mockery in her naked eyes. For, as with everything exciting in this world, the monkeys' fucking is both repulsive and stimulating. The monkeys screech. She gasps. The monkeys stare at her breathlessly. One of them winks. She winks back.

....

I did not die. The truth is, I wanted to bring myself into the picture. To be a protagonist, a hero: to be fallible. Yes, it should have happened: I should have died. I would have liked that. But the cunt basked in the limelight, and my mock-sacrifice went unnoticed.

The only reason I go on is that I know full well that if things get too scary, I can always kill her off. Don't all creators dream of killing their characters in order to save themselves? I can't lose.

....

ZOO PART IV (CONTINUED)

Ela stands in front of another cage, watching baboons fuck. She feels an irrepressible certainty that her cunt will come here, attracted by the spring fever. And at the same instant, she also feels jealous of the baboons, of their bulging, puckered soft assholes which remind her of enlarged vaginas. She thinks: Can I participate in this miracle? Can I join in? Typically, the busy heated baboons interrupt their frantic loud fucks to stare at her dumbstruck from their ascetic enclaves. They can't take their beady eyes off Ela. Now

Ela recognises that expectant look. They want love! Adventure! She knows these faces.

It is in the baboon cage, right now, I see it, spanking the monkeys, literally! It is jumping excitedly from baboon to baboon. I must track it down! This is my chance to get the full scoop.

SIX MONTHS AGO (FLASHBACK)

Ela has changed her mind about what happened to her departed cunt. From the downward curve of her sexual passion factor, Ela deduced that the lens had not been her cunt, but an impostor, strategically placed in an identical jar to fool her. After her initial fascination, her interest in having sex with the lens dwindled to zero. This was clearly not her cunt. And photographs of any sort could not possibly replace her sorely missed physical orgasms.

It seemed no longer relevant to understand the nature of a lens that had been in her life only for a few hours, when she had not understood the workings of a cunt that she had lived with all her life. So she simply treated it as yesterday's lover. Like her cunt, her lens had been a delusion; a snare; a cobweb. She was glad to be rid of it.

Ela decided that the mystery lens was a foil to keep her occupied and unsuspicious, while her real cunt was stolen. An ingenious thief must have abducted her cunt when she was not looking. But 'whodunit'?

Someone who at this very moment was laughing at Ela, screaming in the throes of ecstasy with her cunt. She sat there, knowing her defenceless cunt was getting raped. But there was little Ela could do.

How did one go about relocating a stolen cunt? Would the charge of the robbery and rape of her cunt stand in a court of law? If Ela's mind did not consent to the intercourse, did it matter that she wasn't physically connected with her cunt? Was her cunt Ela's possession even after its removal? Did it lawfully belong to anyone who found it? Couldn't anyone claim that it copulated willingly? She would have to prove the theft. She would have to prove it belonged to her. She would need a lawyer. She would have to go from court to higher court to highest court to establish a precedent. She pictured the headlines: STOLEN CUNT. NOT INSURED. FEARS OF MORE ASSAULTS. IS THERE A CUNT-THIEF RUNNING LOOSE? It was unimaginable. She'd better write it off.

Or should she hire a detective? Call a psychic? Was there a governmental agency that dealt with such complaints? A clearing house? If only her cunt was a pet or something nice, she could advertise for it in the papers and on posters: LITTLE CUNT LOST *à la* Blake.

She hoped the thief would eventually blackmail her. But what if he leased it out or made plaster casts of it to sell to tourists as they do in Hong Kong? Could she survive without it? Who would she be without her cunt? She'd have to learn to live with boredom like other people.

Ela forgot the deranged fire, the mania and lunacy of her wily cunt as it rose and fell in its own froth. She imagined her cunt now helpless, more fragile than a newborn, completely unable to express itself. She felt the sweet maternal exasperation of constantly having to run after an innocent and restless child. But 'whodunit'?

....

I confess: I stole the tricky specimen. I simply had to examine it further. To vivisect it, to wrench from it that innermost secret. I took that cunt under my jurisdiction. It was the only way.

I did change the cunt for an old lens — the symbolism of it moved me deeply — on that day it was scooped out. I only wanted to obtain a thorough understanding of that marvellous cunt while I had the incredible chance. Busy taming my thrashing prisoner,

I shared Ela's confusion at the supernatural qualities of the lens. I had not planned on them. Seeing her unusual photos, I began to suspect that the cunt could be in two places at once; or else that either what I held, or what Ela had photographed, was a mirror reflection.

Soon after, the original cunt fled. Here is the sorry tale:

I took its temperature, measured its dimensions, analysed its texture and consistency. I held a candle under it and watched the flames eat at it. Sex with fire would be the perfect ending for this cunt, I thought then. But before dissecting it, I decided to fuck it first. It was an experience I could not deny myself or science. I was eager to enter a cunt unshackled by the confines of a body. Especially this cunt.

But at that point, I realised that the stupendous cunt was – still? – alive. It was slipping and sliding out of my hold like a poisonous snake. Initially it grew into a long thick staff, a lumpish, blindly inquisitive penis that encapsulated all the loneliness of my humiliation and the mordant comic perspective of my miserable efforts.

I was not intimidated. I held on to it, though I was in shock. It split into writhing stems, like an octopus's tentacles. I grasped it tighter. It changed into a jerking ink-shooting squid, a squirming mouse, a cockroach. I became determined to get to the bottom of it. When it eventually turned back to its original shape, it was still stretching itself into abstract shapes like living silly putty, ranging in colours from green to blue to pink to silver, like an angry face.

I persisted, more curious than ever. I played sexy watery music – Jarre's Equinox – on Ela's CD and lowered the lights, hoping to seduce it. I set it up against her pillows and tried to penetrate it, but I encountered logistic failures. I am one-dimensional when it comes to these things. Due to its volatile state, I had to hold it steady under one hand and position it correctly with the other. It was not easy to keep it still under my control. The very second I put it down to attempt some further adjustments in that precarious setup, the protean cunt darted off, fleeing my hold with startling speed.

It literally ran off! It did not slide or roll or leap away, but ran upright as if on two tiny invisible feet, like a combo **Alien 1** *and wind-up* **Jolly Jumping Pussy.** *It took countless gingerly steps, like a centipede on speed.*

The most beautiful cunt in the world was running in a confused zigzag direction on Ela's floor like a teething toddler, surprised by its own mobility and still unsure of its mechanics. It veered off left and right, as if chased by a drunken driver attempting to run it down. It resembled a tiny dog mutely yelping and limping quickly away, going off to lick its wounds in privacy. I could not believe my own eyes.

It hid under the bed in less than a second. Once it was out of my sight, it proved impossible to locate in the room or outside. I searched thoroughly for days before I opened the apartment door. I surmised that it slipped through the air-conditioning duct or the bathtub draining pipe. But one way or another, it got out of hand.

For months now, I have abandoned Ela, as I have been methodically searching for her footloose cunt and still making little progress. For how does one find a single stray cunt unleashed in NYC?

....

ZOO PART V (CONTINUED)

Ela asks a big-bellied red-nosed bow-legged fish-blue-eyed lemon-skinned middle-aged green-uniformed guard: 'Have you had any unnatural incidents in your cages lately? I am interested in strange unexplainable sights people have actually witnessed in zoos. I look for a small but noticeable creature, silver or pink. Aren't you the man I am looking for?' She fans herself passionately.

The guard slurps and warbles: 'For twenty years now, Miss; yes; I am Bob; I support the IRA and enjoy sharing my gruesome experiences as a part-time paramedic, but now my heart beats like a bewildered bird as, sexy and comfortable, you smile at me from across the years, inviting me to screw you right here in front of the animals. But what is the use of what I say if the sounds finally touch your half-naked body?' He stops abruptly and resumes only after Ela nods permission.

Bob tells her a story: a beautiful shiny pink insect was bothering the monkeys this week. At first everyone thought it was an expensive wind-up toy that some child threw into the cages; but it did not stop dancing, especially around the mammals' peckers, and when they went to clean the cage, it cunningly slipped away; so the guards modified their conclusions. They agreed it was a tiny slimy frog that had the ability to twist its body into a circle; or else it was an exceptionally agile slug. But when Bob threw salt on it, it didn't disintegrate, as a slug should. Now the zoo workers feared it was a Martian, an alien visitor studying earth life.

But Bob did not believe in the supernatural. Bob was sure it was a tropical insect that arrived on a boat from overseas and found its way to the zoo by instinct. Probably an unknown bug that had not yet been classified in Western annals. He informed the zoo entomologist, but they could not even identify the overall species of the creature.

Only last night, thanks to the zoo authorities' generosity and Bob's watchful eye, was the invader removed from the cages before it did any permanent damage. It took nine men to get it out. Bob and his colleagues succeeded because they knew the creature's Achilles' heel: the zoo hired the services of professional gigolos to entice it away!

The nine hired men stripped, danced and groaned, and thus walked out with it jumping all over them. They bellydanced into a waiting wagon and drove off. The plan was that they should trap it in a special sealed container and deliver it to the biologist in charge of top secret research at Columbia University, but they were never heard of again. The FBI had been alerted, in case they tried to sell the alien for ransom, but their tracks had disappeared under most unusual circumstances. They had made no contact with anyone as yet and were feared to be dead.

'Where can I find it? What is your guess?' Ela interrogates Bob.

In her place, Bob would check out the prisons. These unrestrained creatures usually end up in prison sooner or later, he explains. At his paramedic rounds, he actually caught a rumour that a mini-Linda Lovelace is being passed around in the city jail, causing unprecedented agitation.

'The men's jail?' Ela repeats, in anxious, childlike apprehension, thinking: What will remain of it after all this mishandling? In what shape will it be when I get it back? What strength will it have left?

'What do you expect? Women are too sane to fall for that sex-maniac act. Besides, what use would that hollow thing be to a woman? What would she do with it, wear it around her neck? She'd be choked in a second,' Bob replies, laughing at his own joke.

Ela thinks: So from the zoo, I go to the prison. What company it is keeping now that I am not there to hold the reins! It pushes itself too far. She considers paying first a quick visit to the aquarium, to search for it among the polyps, and jellyfish; or to the Botanical Gardens where it may be hiding among the orchids. But she realises that if her cunt is indeed in jail, it constitutes an emergency she can't postpone. For once, she must prioritise.

She takes the subway back. She likes to travel underground when she is depressed.

....

FIVE MONTHS AGO (FLASHBACK)

Sitting in her loft, sipping Napoleon, Ela had an idea: What if someone had found it, but didn't know where to return it? She should make herself discreetly available to them. Otherwise, she risked losing it out of sheer cowardice. She decided on the simplest, bluntest course: the personals. Since it couldn't have gone off far, she only had to place an ad in the *Village Voice*. She composed:

1. A WOMAN WHO MISSES HER CUNT (too weird). A WOMAN WHO NEEDS A CUNT (sounds like lesbian whine). WOMAN WHOSE CUNT IS LOST (morally?). WOMAN WHO FEELS HER CUNT IS LOST (right on the emotion). WOMAN WHO THINKS HER CUNT LOST FOR EVER (vague and clear, keep it) IS SEARCHING FOR IT (tsk). IS LOOKING FOR THE RIGHT PERSON (be direct). LOOKING FOR THE ONE WHO'S GOT IT. FINDER WON'T REGRET. ANY REWARD NEGOTIABLE.

She dreaded the letters of response. She had to locate an agency to read them for a fee. Ela hates mail, for it reminds her how alone she really is not. She thought: J. Dean received 3,000 fan letters a week for three years after his death. Things could be worse. She thought: Isn't a cunt out of context useless, and vice versa: a woman out of cunt? We can do nothing much apart: I am bound to find it.

2. VERY PARTICULAR (nicely bossy and tough) SENSITIVE (no, only men say that) AC/DC (for safety) ATTRACTIVE (necessary) DISCREET (is that negative?) FRIENDLY (reassuring for novices) SEXY (weak) HORNY (a metaphor) YOUNG FEMALE INVITES (old-worldish) SEEKS PERSONABLE (flatter the beast) UNATTACHED WHITE SUPER-TIGHT CUNT FOR SEXY FUN (and deaths) AND LONGTERM RELATIONSHIP. MY PAD. (I'll go to the end of the world, but what's the use of advertising?) FEES ACCEPTABLE.

....

An awkward, balding CEO in a blue blazer, grey flannels, Brooks shirt, pink polka-dot tie, and Yorx SFI AM/FM stereo sunglasses on his eyes making him look like Gregor Samsa, welcomes Ela into the train.

He nods his head right and left continuously like a loosened jack-in-the-box. He interlocutes: 'Do you get car sick often?' He leans against the metal pole, struggling to balance his leather briefcase-cum-generator between his legs, while using a Pioneer portable mini-compact stereo TV, a Zenith Supersport portable computer with a scanner, a MC50 Ricoh portable photocopier with IM.F portable fax, a Futrex 1000 that reads body-fat content, a RC605 Denon pocket microscope, and a Sony mini-recorder digital diary-calculator-data-bank, all connected directly to the briefcase. The above gadgets hang from his arms limply, in a graceless way that reminds Ela of the British Queen carrying her purse in public. They clash, clatter and clang in rude cacophony, as he rocks with the motion of the train. Every few seconds, he feels his back pants pocket for his wallet.

It is this hyper-cramped man who offers Ela his assistance as she gingerly steps on the train and, dragging all his vulgar fetishes with him, sits next to her in order to show her the core of his life. He calls it 'O': an Olympus camera with 1950s design, old-fashioned flash and smooth aluminium body. 'I use this,' he confides, producing an 8mm micro-camera from a pocket, 'but O is my great love!' 'I read her story,' Ela assures him. 'No class, but she has a lovely sense of timing.' He takes down copious notes on his Akai dictaphone as she speaks.

He tells her: 'I'm a pillager of the American Dream, I operate as invisibly as possible. I'm a medievalist by training, a rapist by inclination and a sleazy raider by vocation. You and I are on the same frequency. I look at you, and I feel wired. I don't know about you, but this is a first for me. I suddenly have the urge to measure myself against phallic earth-tone linebacker-size men, to tussle with boxing legends and bash together the heads of love slaves tonguing my nipples. I feel in sync! I am ready to wrestle with big blather! What lies behind the "I"? Are our personalities constructed around a void like an empty suit of armour or is there an archetypal pair of eyes peering through every mask? Do I even exist at this very minute?'

He punches his mini-keyboard, and then invites Ela for drinks on the 1st of April, which is 11 days, 16.5 hours, 12 minutes and 16.07 seconds away. Two minutes and 31 seconds after the CEO's portable generator batteries run out, Ela finally gets off the subway car.

As the subway car roars away, it lets loose a blast of hot air that whistles its way into Ela's gaping orifice. She thinks: If only I had something down there, anything, even a pea, not just an open empty space, I wouldn't feel so exposed! This confirms to her the absolute necessity of locating her cunt at her next destination.

She charges off, expecting to find her cunt behind bars.

....

This morning, six months to date from the decunting day, Old Man the Knife was released from jail. No charges were pressed against him. More to the point, the police lacked evidence, victim and weapon.

I was there of course, looking for clues. The streets looked like a leper's skin, dotted with mud falling off in big rotten chunks.

The blind man who, according to my sources, was already revered in Handicapped Power NY circles, did not want to be released and felt discriminated against by the system that paroled him. Angered by the injustice, which he was persuaded reflected directly on his age and his handicap, he had called for a press conference, after having unsuccessfully demanded that his jailers keep him behind bars.

He now spoke passionately to the reporters who held out their mini-recorders at his face: 'Did I not confess to a crime? Am I not responsible for a violent attack against a defenceless fellow human being? Don't I have the right to a fair trial? Don't I deserve the strictest sentence under the law, as I do not have the excuse of being blinded by rage or circumstance? Am I not a public menace? Why am I discharged like a second-rate citizen, a worthless invalid? Was mine not an imaginative, unique unprecedented crime? Committed without logic, or monetary gain for myself, out of sheer raw badness, in cold blood? Excision for the sake of excision? Isn't America outraged? I refuse to be a threat to society only because this society is blinded to the danger I represent! I do not want to have to prove myself again! I did what I had to do, as a man, and now I am ready to take what is coming to me. I challenge the Public Defender to shut me up!'

He refused to answer questions about the object, or body part, that had, or had not, fallen out of the girl on to the street, and was carried away in secret. He claimed he had no right to speak about the crime, as that would be invading his victim's privacy. All he did was a clear-cut mutilation, he did not expect anything from the victim in return. He did not want to be rewarded or thanked. He only wanted to pay his dues. No, he didn't know where the victim could be contacted.

At first, the crowd, attracted by the presence of microphones and cameras, combed their hair and squeezed to get within camera range, hoping someone would point a lens at them, like a hand gun, and hoot: 'You feel good . . . Give me your lips, your eyes . . . sideways . . . Come closer . . . You love it . . . Beautiful', like James Brown crouched over a Nikon F2.

But soon the crowd had given up on its fantasies and was fed up. They might as well catch this in the comfort of their homes on the 11 o'clock news, colourised and edited down. A hot-dog vendor protested: 'This country is just too damn permissive. We can't give people the right to withhold the truth from the public. It's a crime against the mild-mannered citizen who wants to know what occurs in his community. Congress must enact a law that forces everyone to answer any questions we, the taxpayers, find fit!' The crowd nodded tepidly and quickly dispersed, leaving behind it a gap.

MEN'S CENTRAL JAIL PART II (CONTINUED)

Ela perseveres through a winding, grimy tunnel until she reaches the connecting train that will take her to the state jail.

The subway is crowded: it is lunchtime rush hour in spring. The car reeks with syrupy perfumes, rebellious body odours and dissatisfied hormones. The passengers wear motley uncoordinated combinations of cabbage green, yellow or pink, and sneakers. They remind Ela of Mardi Gras on vacation islands when the locals dress up and act as tourists.

An oily-haired, big-nostrilled, large-crotched Puerto Rican cups his groin as if to protect it and fixes his narrow eyes on her – missing – cunt. He looks like Charles Casagemas in Picasso's *La Vie*. He pushes through the passengers who stand upright and uptight with their steaming bodies in rocking contact, reading bestsellers and tabloids watchfully and fantasising about each other, and bends into Ela's ear.

He says: 'Chiquita, you're a woman up for grabs. For myself, I love music but I avoid it. It makes me aware of time, getting old, but I love it 'cause it says nothing. It's all looks!' He stands so close to Ela that his crotch touches her mouth. Ela thinks: I am not into this. The Puerto Rican: 'Yes, you are! You're the true land of opportunity. Your pussy sings to me. I've got a running sore in my crotch. Sex really wounds me.' Ela: 'You smell like a baboon.' The Puerto Rican, still looking where her cunt should be: 'Does that make you feel all juicy? I'm a very emotional guy, *mujer*. My name is Olegario.' He shouts to be heard over the noise of the train; his putrid breath burns her cheek, his hard pelvis burns her chin in a Bergmanesque close-up. Ela: 'I only fuck mute men. So sorry.'

She gets up and squeezes away from him. She dashes forth using her elbows as rudders. Hands sneak up on her and sour breaths are exhaled into her nostrils. She keeps her mouth firmly shut. Bodies fidget, stir and fuss and many feet step on hers and she steps on many feet. Her cap falls off her head, her cape gets caught in zippers.

She reaches the gap between cars, leans back on the rattling sliding door with her cheek against the graffiti and shuts her eyes. She still can't breathe. She feels a hot and slimy throbbing slug gnaw at her underbelly. It may be the Puerto Rican. At that, she faints.

....

FOUR MONTHS AGO (FLASHBACK)

I had not had a lead for weeks in my pursuit of Ela's cunt.

I was waiting for the subway train on my way back from the pier. I happened to glance down, and I saw the cunt lying near my feet! It was flapping about on the dirty yellow line, neglected, dusty, unnoticed, playing with the remnants of a Butterfinger candy bar, screwing itself around it and jumping about like a gay kitten, stained with black coal and melted chocolate. My heart broke at the sight. In my excitement, I took a step towards it and said: 'Let me help you!' I plunged towards it certain that this time it could not escape. The poor devil was trapped between my advancing feet, positioned so they could raid it from every side, and the edge of the platform.

In that instant, slowly as if sorrowfully, the cunt rolled off the platform. I jumped forward, eager to save it, but then staggered. The headstrong cunt was hanging from the parapet, planning to fall into the tracks. I hollered: 'No!' Like a latter-day Madame Bovary, it was threatening to jump in front of the 8th Avenue Express and be brutally cut up by the train!

I stopped dead. I had plenty of indication that it was unaware of its own worth. It might easily kill itself in self-defence, on my account. That I could never bear. I was afraid if I took the remaining step, it would let go of its hold and throw itself into the tracks to be squashed into jello by the train whose lights I saw light up the dark mouth of the tunnel. I retreated without taking my eyes from it, hoping it would climb into the subway car where I could catch it. But when the train stopped and its doors opened, the wanton cunt disappeared under the avalanche of feet rushing in and out of the doors.

I made a quick decision. I judged it to be unable, because of its size, to hop over the gap into the car. I gambled on its exhaustion, which I assumed led it to contemplate its own self-extinction, and I lost. When the doors shut, the recalcitrant cunt was nowhere in sight. No deformed silver mass lay among the tracks, no wet silver trail flowed on the grime. Did someone kick it accidentally into the car? Did it climb on to the shoe of a passenger who struck its fancy? Now that I had more time to think, all these other possibilities occurred to me. For the first time, I began to question my skills.

The cunt, not I, is the gap at the centre of this world, where everything is sucked in and spewed back out till the end of time, I suddenly realised with fear. No one else knew this.

....

MEN'S CENTRAL JAIL PART III (CONTINUED)

Ela comes to, lying on the subway floor, her skull bouncing up and down on the metal. Her feet are held high up by the Puerto Rican and a thin bland woman in white plastic fur and caked Doctor Ruth blush. Ela thinks: Whenever I faint, people lift my skirts and take a peek. I lose consciousness, they raise my legs. It must be instinct. They must think it's my cunt that causes me to faint, so they air it.

Suddenly someone slaps her. Someone else drenches her with Coke. Someone else forces a jelly bean through her teeth. Someone fans her with a Harlequin romance. Someone sprays her with dime scent. They're coming at her from all sides. Her pupils disappear, her mouth twitches. The disgusting taste in her mouth reminds Ela of old men's cum.

The women leaning over her with concern resemble wilting greens, frozen vegetables. A squash in orange lipstick, baby-blue eyeshadow and frightening Divine hairdo explains to all present: 'She is having an epileptic fit; I teach elementary school so I've seen the symptoms. You can buy medication now for this kind of thing.' An overdressed bag-lady in flannel robe and old men's slippers – a tomato – nods: 'I'm a kook. You a kook too?' A shrivelled okra with skeletal torso, anorexic limbs, hollow cheeks, in xs-Levis and shoulderless top: 'My father-in-law gets these spells from diabetes. She needs an insulin shot.' A potato in a lamé business suit: 'Maybe she is a Pentecostal.'

An antiquated artichoke with bleached hair, black-pencilled brows, purple-coloured plaited lips and a florid polyester dress pitches in: 'I just read about this woman who gave birth to nine monkeys and she was passed out all through pregnancy. It's front page today. We better warn this girl she's pregnant.' A carrot-lady adds: 'I think she is on a twelve-step programme.' A cucumber with long legs, a terry-cloth dress and high pumps: 'No. My grandpa has Parkinson's, like the woman in *On Golden Pond*, and he acts like this, shaking and falling down all the time. I can't stand being around him.' This comment gives birth to a heated exchange on the nature of assorted diseases and relatives.

Ela manages to lower her legs. She embraces the metal pole, wraps her legs around it and convulses. She thinks: Something in the centre of the stage is rotting. I'm paralysed like Hamlet. I'm an albatross.

She smells the display of sneakers crowded around her, as she hears an unnaturally hot breath in her ear: 'You've got an electric hot stinging pussy, not a magpie or anything. I'd love you even as a dead carcass.' Olegario. Seldom has Ela perceived such sadness. She turns to the nearest sneaker and throws up. This creates an uproar.

The commuters hang on to neighbours' sleeves and purses and laps, make grimaces of exaggerated disgust, hold their noses although it is impossible to smell anything amidst the perfumes and sweat. Even those who were only stealing glances at her before, in hopes of being themselves stared at, now face with fear Ela's silver vomit that rolls and slides around following the jerky movements of the train. They point to it wide-eyed and mutter plosives as if they were standing in a low-budget 1960s film staring out at the UFO on their lawn. They climb on the seats to save themselves. A narrow space opens around her shiny excretion: the desired corridor via which Ela makes once again her way out.

She heads for the nearby booth, out of which pokes the head of a uniformed conductor who announces the names of approaching stations in an unintelligible jargon and every so often looks over the passengers with the pompous proprietary authority of a medieval landowner who inspects his live cargo. There she hopes to be temporarily protected.

A black man in a blue uniform a few sizes too tight for him questions Ela in a brutal city accent: 'Did God tear you out of heaven with his teeth and spit you out?' Ela: 'I can't breathe.' Conductor: 'I am Wendell. I want to sit with you in a field of daisies.' Ela: 'Can I sit here?' Conductor: 'You've dealt me a mortal blow.' Ela: 'Could you move over a bit?' Conductor: 'I don't mean to crowd you. You blast me and leave me blind. I want to be blind, I want to be blasted, I don't want it to be any different. Where you from? Where do you live? Are you married? Are you straight? How long are you staying here? What is this perfume you wear? Have you ever been to a baseball game? Do you like blueberry pancakes for Sunday breakfast?'

....

THREE MONTHS AGO (FLASHBACK)

I got out of a cab on 42nd Street. I slowly made my way

through the sex arcades, going from one peep show to the next, looking at pussies and searching for inspiration. I entered a booth on a hunch.

The walls of this viewing booth were covered with dull brown pantry-style wallpaper, as if the owners wanted to make the voyeurs feel at home. The only thing missing was a spraying of imitation-scent mother's cooking. Even the wastebasket, presumably there to receive any discharge, was lined with the pastoral wallpaper. A minuscule decrepit sign read: SEXUAL ACTIVITY PROHIBITED. The slot held up to ninety-nine coins, but after some tries, I grew impatient.

Then suddenly I saw it! I was stunned but certain: it was on top of the vagina of a bulbous jiggly nude Roseanne lookalike. There it lay, exposed behind the filthy glass of the two-way mirror, in a dingy booth on Times Square. I could never mistake its silver sheen, the incessant plucking of the lips that formed a circle exhaling and then snipping again, or the dreamy fog that gave it the shifty appearance of a mirage. I put in one more of the special gold-painted peep-show coins with an eye engraved on them, just to make sure. It was it!

My experienced eye distinguished the frizzy edges of the broader, darker, flatter vagina underneath. Ela's cunt sat on it as on a dish. There was no harmony between the fake overacted caresses the hired woman bestowed on her body and the fluid authentic electrified movements of 'her' horny cunt. They were miles apart in quality and quantity.

What was the cunt doing there, taking over the place of other women's genitals, showing itself off shamelessly to any undersexed passerby? Fraud! It was traumatic to see that special creature lounging between the ruined legs of a low-class whore hired as a spectacle for a quarter! It was making a fool of me: I couldn't have it, I could only look at it, for as long as I could stand it, for a silly price.

Just like old times, I thought. I ran out of the booth

looking for the manager. But no one would let me in to see the whore in person. I ran back to the screen just as the shutter was closing and put in a new coin to hold on to the view for 45 more seconds. The water-baggy whore didn't look lascivious or erotic, but bored or drugged, overfucked and terribly matter-of-fact, even businesslike. Anticlimactic.

Why did our refined cunt ever choose her? I grew mad.

Knowing how close to me it was and yet how unavailable, I began to kick the glass with all my strength, and even threw the festering wastebasket at it. I punched the screen repeatedly, screaming: 'Give that cunt back to me!' It didn't break, but gave in and rebounded, reminding me of the soft glass of Ela's lens; they were probably made of the same obscure, accursed, modern plastic concoction.

The whore immediately ran off and was replaced by a mirror that reflected my rage, and then by hissing static. Out of nowhere a sleek broad-shouldered Korean bouncer jumped on me and hit me in the groin. I felt nothing of course. I was shouting to him about the cunt's story, how I'd pay him as much as he asked if he helped me get that one cunt, which didn't belong to the woman inside the glass, but to humanity, and was running loose, and had to be captured, for the sake of science if nothing else. I might as well have been talking to a monkey: no expression disturbed his blank, pudgy face; he threw me out.

Then in a surprising British accent, he said: 'We don't like your kind here. Better not come back, or I'll call the police. The Mayor, the Governor, the Police Commissioner come here and even they behave.' But I already knew that cunt wouldn't be found at the same spot twice.

And I did fear jail. So I needed a new plan of action. Fast.

MEN'S CENTRAL JAIL PART IV (CONTINUED)

Ela is chatting with a young pock-marked guard at the prison gate who turns out to be Bob the zookeeper's twin. He wears a violet silk scarf around his neck under his uniform and a blue carnation in his chest pocket. He looks off into the distance as he inhales the smoke, squinting with Bogart-like eyes and muses: 'I am a balletomane: I hunger for aromatically musical movement, for tons of frou-frou and costly toe-shoes, for beanstalk ballerinas and their midget tits. Love for me is like dancing asleep. After sex I ask: Must it be like this? I always lock the door before sex. Afterwards I eat like a Roman.' He adds: 'What is "life" in Latin? I used to know it.' Ela: 'Pussy.' His eyes light up and he nods, yes, now he remembers it.

Ela feels like a fraud without her cunt and talk of sex offends her. She tells him she needs information. He tells her his name is Rob. She wonders if there have been any pussy-related incidents recently in his prison; she is researching prison promiscuity for *NOW*. In her loins she can feel her crater coiling in hang-jaw anticipation.

Rob says of course, he's right now in fact getting a hard-on, why, only yesterday a lifer got his cock chewed off, isn't that something, tsk, unimaginable; he doesn't know how, but inmates go through those things all the time, they'll pull anything off, they're maniacs in there; it is impossible to keep up with all the sex hysteria; and the lifer is in the hospital, knocked off. She asks to speak to the victim's cellmate, or to any other prisoner who has been there long and knows all the gossip, a Dick, a Tom, or a Harry. Rob promises to bend some rules and pull some strings for her; all he wants in return is the light from her pussy, he says. She agrees, lying. It is a deal.

Walking off with Rob, Ela wonders when her new conservative sex repulsion first originated. What has happened to her historically renowned quest for the perfect fuck? Gone the way of all good things . . .

....

TWO MONTHS AGO (FLASHBACK)

For weeks I was running to massage parlours, sex clubs, porno-extravaganzas, S&M shows, bondage parades, swingers' groups, sex-aerobics classes. I peered into aqua blue blow-ups in periodicals sold hermetically sealed in plastic, titled Prude, Rapture, Squeeze, Shaved Pussy Special. *I inspected countless pussies peeking through Fredericks' of Hollywood undies or wrinkle-free explorer's garbs. Like the Japanese businessmen around me, I placed $50 bills into sweaty G-strings so that dancers showed me their costly sponge-like vaginas at close range. I watched girls do all kinds of absurd things to themselves, lick their own nipples, suck their own vaginas, push their own fingers up their asses, pretending they were two people fucking. I saw girls whose vaginal muscles were stronger than my pectorals, play ping-pong with their vaginas, smoke with their vaginas, throw a lasso with their vaginas. I saw girls fucking with Dobermans, with clothes-lines, with a machine gun, fucking on stilts or while hanging from chandeliers. I saw hundreds of chains, metal cages, metal cocks, nameless instruments of torture. And I patiently continued to go from porno show to porno film to porno shop, anywhere I could locate an abundance of genitalia and audiences, certain that the cunt couldn't resist that combination.*

I ran into it when I least expected it, of course. I was sitting in an XXX theatre, exposed to the pervasive odours of sailors' cum and unwashed socks and to the prolonged discoloured bleating on the screen. The moment that the soundtrack picked up as if the cavalry were coming and the porno stars repeated: 'Yes', I saw the cunt.

It was sitting a few seats in front of me! I wouldn't have perceived it in the dark if it weren't for its familiar eerie glow that made it look as if it were made of sparkles. I ducked at once so that it wouldn't spot me and lurked in the shadows trying to form a plan.

I noticed then, to my astonishment, that it (or should I at this point say 'she'?) was sitting next to someone who, after some more careful examination, proved to be nothing more than a substantial dick. Yes, loose in the theatre, by itself, a circumsised American dick out on its own! Where did she meet it? Did she abduct it from its owner? Did she sever it to keep her company?

They were sharing the cracked vinyl seat and wildly imitating the fucking as it took place in the film, so that they would hurriedly change positions, and slow down or speed up or curve back in accordance with what was projected on screen as if playing at being the mirror.

The dick showed great talent: it performed the part of every changing position diligently and without for a moment losing its strong upward curve. The cunt, on the other hand, was clearly improvising, writhing when the porno star's vagina remained still, changing rhythm and confusing its ambitious partner, obviously bored by the repetitive missionary position of its movie counterparts. She pirouetted in and out of the pounding dick, spun around it as it penetrated her, undulating her belly, or hole, flirtatiously like a luminous oriental dancer

Even though I had continuously peered at crass sexual imagery and genitals for the past few weeks, I could not control the surge of revulsion that overtook me at the sight of this terrifying obscenity, this mockery. I sat witnessing two unadorned genitals slurp and slosh in a small pool of secretion, fucking blindly on a public plastic seat!

I was surprised by how much the presence of legs, underbellies, waists, arms and heads contributes to, and perhaps even justifies, our interest in, and our tolerance of, sexual conduct. Genitals, I realised, though necessary and even enjoyable, require some sort of seasoning, a few extra touches, to give them the appropriate look; otherwise they are alien and disgusting like obscure protozoa or wormy salivating molluscs that have crawled high up on someone's clean white wall, unnoticed. Oh no, this wasn't a sight of life!

It was now clear to me that the cunt had picked up this separated dick, and perhaps was planning to start a family of similar loose genitalia jerking themselves obliviously into eternity! This time I planned my next move, making certain I wouldn't overreact and lose it.

I rose, walked down the aisle, staring only at the action on the screen as if absorbed by it, hiding my face in my coat collar, until I reached their row and stepped sideways towards them as if to sit next to the mating couple. They were rolling in and out of each other with abandon, and I lost no time: I abruptly sat on them with all my force.

Now I had them trapped! I could feel the romancing genitalia fumbling under my coat, perhaps still unaware of their change of fate, the dick pushing towards the entrance of my buttocks and tickling me. I shook off my trenchcoat, let it fall over my prey under my ass and even tucked the sides under the borders of the seat. Then, once I had made sure they were still squiggling beneath my bottom, I carefully tied my coat ends into a makeshift parcel. I jumped up and pulled my crossed coat sleeves tight. I grabbed the struggling contents of my coat in both hands, turned it upside down so the flat back was underneath and bunched up all the openings. Quickly, joyfully, I ran out.

Now I had her! She was under my bondage! They fought like live cats locked in a bag and about to be drowned. I was in ecstasy!

I stormed into a dilapidated hotel next door, got myself a room, locked the shaky door, checked the stained windows, which luckily were not broken, and threw my derelict package on the unmade bed triumphantly. I was ready to dance, swirl, shout a paean, blow-up the place!

How could I have imagined, after all my precautions, that under the scarlet lining of my coat lay only a single erect dick? Yet that was the spectacle afforded to my eyes as I untied the knot. What could I do? I checked if my coat had been torn by the exposed screws on the movie seat. No! I looked around the room even though I knew I wouldn't find her. Perhaps she had detected me all along and escaped at the very last instant just to enrage me more. Perhaps she turned liquid and trickled out of my trap. All I knew was that she had run off, slipping through my hands again. I had it and yet I didn't have it.

Meanwhile, the excited dick seemed to have no consciousness of its new circumstances. It danced a lonely number on the bed, standing on its wider base, blindly reaching around with its head right and left and upward, hoping to touch a penetrable surface. It had no idea where it was or what it looked like. I was so disappointed that my impulse was to take it out on this poor victim. I admit that I tried to strangle it. I put my hands tightly around it and pressed as hard as I could to choke it. That was a mistake, for the immediate result was a forceful arch of off-white liquid squirting out of its mouth and into my eyes. It occurred to me that I had given it pleasure instead!

Irony upon irony, faux pas after faux pas! I was not made for this plot! I considered, for a moment, giving up. I thought this wriggling, writhing, air-grasping tool was a clear sign. A mirror.

Maybe I could put it in a jar of water, take it to Ela and say: 'Look, use this. Forget womanhood. Be a man. You and I both will start over. With our singular looks, we only need to screw this on and we'll be perfect males too. We can get men's point of view, what they see inside a vagina, why they go mad, all those mysteries. Let's try both sides! Think of Tiresias: you'll be a seer. We can both be blind seers!' I knew I could persuade her. I have that power. That, I was made for. Perhaps there was a moral lesson somewhere here.

MEN'S CENTRAL JAIL PART V (CONTINUED)

In the visitors' gallery at the prison, Ela is shooting the breeze with red-headed hairy dirty Harry through the visitors' window. By now, having shed her cape, cap and sunglasses in the subway, she is left in the tiny red lace dress and pink elfin boots, like a plucked bird. Harry is 6 feet tall and wide like a truck in his threadbare grey uniform.

Ela tells Harry she has come for a clue regarding a cannibal.

Harry says she's come to the right person. He discloses: 'First all of us boys thought it was a pink plastic dildo, I mean *Pocket-Pussy*; but high quality, man, exactly like the real thing; a killer. Someone must have sneaked it in and it was doing the rounds. I've got a love doll called Sheena, sells for £39.95 and has fleshlike extra-thick wet latex labia for a lasting relationship, says the label, but that is nothing in comparison . . . I mean totally high-tech . . . the guys were fighting over it and everything like it was a real broad. So it finally reached Dick, who's the big man here and has got tattoos on his chest that look exactly like that Pocket-Pussy. It turns out, Dick said it was a real-life woman's cunt, on its own . . . what a find . . . and that this was a real man's job so he'd keep it to himself . . . he wanted to sleep with it every night 'cause he said he'd never screwed anything so tight . . . this is the best fucking cunt in the world you jerks, he said . . . and Dick's had pussy from all over . . . he's done hundreds of pussies from every town and country . . . said he'd let us watch and jerk off but that was all . . . he punched Tom's eyes out for asking to borrow it . . . he ordered "no talk with Rosie!" That was final . . . maybe they knew each other from before. Dick is a smart little pig, but Tom said to me secretly this thing will ruin Dick, he'll fall, it's like a man's calling to love one broad once for good and this was it for Dick . . . so Dick kept it on a string all day, a wire or rope or something, I dunno, like a bird, a chick . . . and said to us all "Rosie this" and "Rosie that" . . . in the mornings he called out "I've got a live one here!" and laughed . . . he let it free at night to screw . . . he'd stick it in and be screaming crazy "fucking hell, I'm God!" . . . he kept the jail up . . . everyone was jerking off . . . I've never heard a man come for so long . . . we thought they'd have him removed to the madhouse or shoot him up to shut him up . . . but I guess they liked to listen too . . . until the fourth night that he had it. Now that was weird. Just dead silent all of a sudden. We couldn't get a peek because we were locked up; but this guard says Dick tried to fuck it but it was slipping out of Dick's fists like a live eel, water snake, it wouldn't stay put. It shook and squirmed like the devil, but you don't know Dick — he held it hard and went in, all the way. Then it happened. Blood and all. Dick being tough, bit his tongue off and didn't utter a sound. They found him half dead. The guard had passed out too. The creepy thing had gone off on its own, just like that, carrying along old Dick's cock.'

Ela suddenly feels as if she's ogling at a peep show on Times Square, with Harry looking more like Roseanne. She realises: No one here has playful eyes. Harry, bringing her back to real time: 'The Doc searched the toilets and they asked us all if we saw it but Dick's cock vanished with Rosie. Who knows where! Reno, for all my guess is worth. Having a screwball. My notion is, the cops should shoot it, or else it'll put a lot of our guys out of use. You can't bite off a man's cock and run off with it like nothing happened!' Ela: 'Don't they want it alive?' Harry: 'Who can trust it? You've no idea how good it is! I'm talking heady stuff.' Ela: 'I must find it. Who is the guard who saw it? Where can I go next?' Her voice sobs.

Harry: 'The guard has been off duty since, maybe he's having nightmares or getting drunk or whatever, it shook him up. My theory is, it's killed a dick! Check out the women's. If it's a cunt, that's where they'd take it, if they caught it. But if they wait to fry it in the chair, it'll do much damage yet. Once a cunt, always a cunt, I say. They better not let it in back here, I'm telling you. We'll lynch it like they used to, give it what it deserves this time, tear that hole apart. We'll fuck that sucker, in the name of dead Dick!'

....

I threw away from me the miserable sticky dick that had shrunk in my vengeful hands to the size of an earthworm. I had tried all I could in the hard-sex arena, and here was the sad result. As I left the seedy hotel, I threw the dick into a Salvation Army collection basket. All dicks look incredibly old when limp, I noticed. Perhaps somebody else had a need for this antique.

I was obsessed with that cunt. I saw nothing but its wet smirk around me. The harder the search, the more excited I became. I entertained no more thought of a truce. I wanted an unconditional surrender. The cunt was my nemesis. My failure only gave me more reason to look for it everywhere. For me, this was a pilgrim's progress.

....

Ela is going to the women's prison. It is early evening, visiting hours are over, the wind is blowing hysterically and Ela has begin to stoop already. But she can't afford to wait another day, or hour, if her cunt is in such serious trouble. She must catch up with it.

Anxious to avoid all time-consumming communication, she scribbles a note on her knees and holds it up at the first crossroads. It reads: I'M CATHOLIC. I'VE MADE A VOW NOT TO SPEAK TO ANY MAN NOR HEAR A MAN'S VOICE FOR A YEAR. A HOLY VOW TO ST BARBARA. PLEASE HELP ME KEEP IT. IT IS TO SAVE MY DEVOUT SISTER, WHO IS DYING FROM UNKNOWN DISEASE. I MUST NOT BE TEMPTED. MAY THE GRACE OF ST BARBARA BE WITH YOU.

She looks out in the characteristic composed-and-absent way of the deaf. She knows that if she makes people feel like heroes in a world full of love, she can be safe and expedient.

As expected, the note instantly performs the miracle. A cabbie slams his brakes, beams, and breaks into a radiant smile from hairy ear to hairy ear like a proud simple-minded father. She slides in the car and jots down her next destination. He continues to smile throughout the trip, blinking his eyes sweetly in the rear-view mirror.

'From jail to jail, huh?' he comments, through the foggy window that separates them. He has the hearty chagrin of an immigrant whose dreams have been undone by the constant drip of fatigue. He wears a brown oily suit and a black velveteen tie with Elvis painted on it, which hangs loosely around his soiled collar with a knot so tight and old it is the size of a pea; he evidently prefers to pull his beloved tie over his head rather than untie it. He has a nose like the prow of a ship, lidless brown eyes, an alcoholic's dry skin, a black-smith's shoulders and his nails are beaten to the roots. He tells himself:

'How unusual to find someone who still believes these days! This semi-naked girl is the first saint I meet in person. I mustn't speak, or God knows what blasphemies might come out of me. She is a nice-looking vehicle, someone to tear up the night with. But this is my chance to do a favour for God. She will go far, this funny-looking pretty holy punk! Maybe she will be Mother Theresa one day! And the poor sister, how lucky to be loved like this!' He imagines every detail of her heart-breaking story that she would otherwise have to invent herself. Now at last, Ela can take a nap on the back seat.

....

TWO MONTHS AGO (FLASHBACK)

I covered museums, department stores, Broadway shows and discos, calculating that the cunt must take the route of any person alone for the first time in the city, not in order to acclimatise itself but to seduce the naive victims it has a fondness for. I took the Staten Island ferry, amidst sleepy commuters and wide-eyed tourists shouting and shooting all at once. Click! Click! Those sounds took me back to that hard September day that ended so disastrously, but I hoped those very sounds would attract the cunt. So I suffered the proximity of picture-crazy lenses directed thoughtlessly in my direction, and eventually came to see a smirking cunt in every lens that snapped near me. I reminded myself I had to stay firm and relentless until I stepped foot on mound f/32 and planted my flag into it.

On my ninth visit to the mammoth ungraceful statue, I finally saw it! What a surprise it afforded me! It was posing between Liberty's colossal legs, splat against the bronze dress at the spot where the foot-long iron vagina of the Lady would have been inserted if she were not a puritan. It flickered proudly over the river wastes, reflecting the light, shining like a mirror, like a movie star. It was delighted to be photographed by the awed tourists. Beaming out like a precarious lighthouse, Liberty's cunt looked over NYC like a conqueror! The sea wind blew through its folds, making it flap like an American flag.

I climbed Liberty's endless stairs as if running for my life. At the corresponding floor, I looked through a smutty window and saw: nothing. It was gone. This hide and seek in which the deceitful cunt had all the odds in its favour was beginning to exhaust me.

I wondered: Is it possible that it will continue to go by unseen by everyone else? If everyone wasn't blinded by habit and decorum, it would be caught at once. What can a single sluggish and flat observer like me achieve? I trudge after it, but I am not built to be active. Oh, if only people understood that this is not a metaphor!

Ela opens her eyes to a grim reality: her cunt is an angel. A silver halo hovers over its lips and it wears thin white wings, like a lepidopteron. It sits alone on a huge gold-studded throne. A white pigeon that looks like the Holy Spirit flies into the cunt's lips, which snap shut at once. The pigeon flaps its wings and expires.

[PAN TO] Bellydancers with slanted eyes dressed in silver and gold gauzes that flow as their bodies undulate, and tall eunuchs with tiaras, heavily embroidered vests, thick lips and fat colourful birds, probably parrots, perched on their shoulders; they crisscross the room bearing golden trays laden with masks, eyepatches, diaphragms, cameras and little cards that read: I HAVE MADE A VOW NOT TO SPEAK OR HEAR. PLEASE HELP ME. It rains a gold dust that whirls in the silent wind.

A gong is mutely sounded. A curtain goes up to reveal Ela tied down to her bed like a naked Gulliver. Grotesquely made-up nude children climb on her. A little girl straddles her face. Ela sees a knife protrude out of the bald infantile vagina. She forces Ela to give the knife a blowjob. Ela recognises the knife: it's the one that decunted her. She can't move; the blade slides between her lips; it is cutting out her mouth. Ela can't make a sound; because her tongue is severed.

Her cherubic cunt is laughing with evident abandon, opening its lips wide, vibrating like a rocking robin. Luckily there is no sound.

[SOUND EFFECT: Car *screeching* to a halt] They have arrived at the jail. As Ela wakes up, she checks for any TV in the cab: no. It was a dream.

The servile, happy driver opens her door, bowing and glowing. His primeval smell pervades her. A smile is now permanently on his face, as if glued on it. He says: 'Please, I want no money for the ride; I'm so moved by your story, I want to be a part of it.' At once he realises with shame that he is not supposed to speak according to her vow, covers his mouth with his calloused hand and shakes his finger as in 'bad, bad!' He then shakes his head right and left, opens his arms up from the elbows and shakes them left to right, and his entire body motions one non-stop 'No!' his head pointing toward the meter.

Ela nods and smiles humbly. She is terrified to speak herself and test the virtual reality of her oral castration. She turns towards the prison gates, summoning her courage to address the guard on duty. But before she can get a word out, the uniformed bulky woman shuts the gates in her face: 'After hours.' Ela feels like a mousetrap has been clamped to her mouth. She furtively looks behind her.

The cabbie is waving at her, clasping his hands together, upwards, in a handshake with himself, like a coach outside the boxing ring.

....

'And I wonder, why, why, why, she ran away, my little runaway, my run, run, run, run, runaway . . .' *The sounds of the world going by bombard me with references to that cunt, Pandora's box, which I seek with the madness of a romantic young Werther.*

....

WOMEN'S CENTRAL JAIL PART III
(CONTINUED)

Ela thinks: Once upon a time, I could have used my cunt to get what I needed. Now I must depend on words. What torture! She pleads with the guard: she's come on the recommendation of Bob and Rob, no, she does not want to see a prisoner, but she must see the director.

The gates open laboriously but close sharply and fast behind her. This prison seems to Ela more austere, cold, drab, dangerous. She is led into the imposing building to a room crowded with hundreds of women, inmates and guards, all glued immobile to a TV set. They are watching a *Hard Copy* special on promiscuity in the women's prison.

Ela stares at all the tight-tongued women vengefully. In her mind she pictures herself stealing their cunts, cutting them out quietly, freezing them, pickling them, drying them, wearing them each alternatively, changing into two or three different cunts in the course of a fuck, or exchanging them – at a ratio of 100 for 1 – for her own.

Ela is introduced to the warden, an anorexic platinum blonde in a Paul Poiret chiffon uniform and Salvatore Ferragamo heels, with ruby lips and diamond earrings who moans: 'You're a striking woman. Do you need my advice? Let me ask you first: Do you need a martini?'

She leads Ela to her office. There is a Tamara de Lempicka on the wall, an old gramophone, and a Louis Vuitton octagonal beauty case on the spotless desk. They sit down to discuss Ela's plight.

The anorexic jailer: 'Food makes me feel guilty like a criminal.' Ela: 'Have you been to San Blas? When women get their first period they paint their faces black. The dye stays on for a year. I'll do that tonight, cover my face with ashes. I'll hold a candle under the mirror.' Anorexic jailer: 'I had a Mexican gal here who'd known Castaneda, and she explained to me why food is poisonous.' Ela: 'I was in the sauna in Santa Barbara when a Mexican labourer peeked in and sank his infected teeth into my cunt on impulse. It was a nice surprise.' Anorexic jailer: 'I cannot even begin to picture what happens to food inside us. Were you naked?' Ela: 'He must have come to clean the pool.' Anorexic jailer: 'Love is our habit of saying: "Give me from your mouth to eat." As the Hunger Artist in my past life I was happier, proud inside that cage. Since then I keep having to prove my innocence by not being burned when I put my face into a bowl of hot soup and not drowning when thrown in with a stone on my neck.' Ela: 'Love is my carving board; it's an accessory.'

They sit across each other, like thin-lipped tough-talking broads in a *film noir*, exchanging words that are bullets from their hearts. The anorexic jailer pats her hair, which reminds Ela of the Caribbean sand and which looks painted on her skull. She keeps her cheek under her other hand throughout their talk as if concealing lesions on her face. She moves minimally.

Anorexic jailer: 'If I were writing about you, I would say: Something in her denies participation.' Ela: 'I do enjoy undressing in front of old paralytic men in wheelchairs and lying naked at their feet to sunbathe. The impossible turns me on.' Anorexic jailer: 'I would be happy if it was impossible for me to go to the bathroom and evacuate; that function disturbs me profoundly. During work, I often fall on the ground screaming, frothing from the orifices.' Ela: 'I've come to ask you for an orifice. A prisoner of yours.' Anorexic jailer: 'Did you say Orpheus? I believe it was a brand name in antiquity. I am not a good consumer. I stick my middlefinger into each hole to stop the flow, but this corroding liquid is everywhere. I dream of plugging up all the holes. I feel it flow out of my pores in my sleep.'

Ela: 'I know; I must find her before it's too late. I was told she came here because she bit some cock off.' Jailer: 'But that's common practice. I'll check the files. What name does she go by?' Ela: 'She's generally called a cunt.' Jailer: 'Is that her Christian name?' Ela: 'Oh well, she's wet, petite, tense, very quiet but she likes a lot of action.' Jailer: 'Is she the one who just went on hunger strike? Wait here. Please don't eat anything.'

....

A MONTH AGO (FLASHBACK)

I needed to pore over the information I had gathered to discern a pattern that would enable me to predict the cunt's next escapade and to be there waiting for it with my net spread open. So I walked into Ray's World Famous Pizza and ordered a slice of eggplant and cheese. My glance took in a short cook singing off-key in his native language and making a show for the pedestrians of throwing the round dough up in the air and rolling it to make the crust. It shimmered in the light but as I am not a pizza expert, I kept my suspicions at bay.

I paid, laid my steaming paper plate on the linoleum counter and tried to concentrate. But the silver light was too piercing by then and too familiar. Could it be what I thought? Could it have grown to such proportions? For the dough twirling around in the air in front of the open window was clearly much wider than the cunt Ela and I had known. Yet its beckoning light could never be mistaken. That bright cunt was screwing up my life again, stirring me up even at my lunch!

I wanted to shout 'There is a cunt on that pizza!' but I didn't have the guts. Only on these pages can I truthfully describe what I've seen. Maybe some time, I could make a true-story TV movie about it all.

I coolly walked up to the small, eager cook and began a conversation on the nature of his job, how long he'd done it, where had he learned, did he like it, it looked so difficult and yet such fun to throw the dough up in the air and catch it, like a frisbee, or juggling, I'd love to try it, could I really give it a spin? He was flattered, unsuspicious. He looked around to see if more customers envied his talent now that public interest was peaking.

My hands were shaking. I knew I had to hold on to it no matter how slippery it would be and how smooth I was, and run away with it at once.

But a new shock awaited me. 'This one,' he said in a squealing accent, 'is ready; you ruin it; so we start a fresh one.' And without further ado he laid it on a black rusty tray and smothered it with grated mozzarella. I shouted: 'No!' The customers froze at the roar of my voice; some pedestrians ran in. People got up from their seats to watch and help me.

'Don't do it!' I repeated in the same shrill voice, unable to imagine how the cunt would escape being grilled and consumed for $2.99 a slice, but equally unable to explain to people mechanically performing their menial jobs that they were about to ruin the most valuable cunt in the world. I felt a burning pain in my own groin.

If I dashed to save it, I would be arrested and locked up in an asylum no doubt. So I held myself in check and watched them complete their funeral ritual, cover it with wreaths of onions and garlands of shredded peppers, submerge it in thick tomato sauce and bury it with a long shovel deep in the cavernous Erebus of their ovens. I broke into silent tears.

Later I bought the whole delicious-smelling pizza and took it home. I spent hours searching through the gooey strands for any silver slivers. I found nothing in the least unusual in it. I had just watched my cunt being burnt at the stake. I always expected that would happen. I forced myself to eat the whole thing. I spent the day feeling sick.

In the end, exhausted and hating myself, I resolved to burn my manuscript, turned on the TV, and fell asleep in the bathtub.

....

WOMEN'S CENTRAL JAIL PART IV
(CONTINUED)

The anorexic jailer returns with the TV set. She says: 'It's not here any more. I sent the girls to sleep; I'm afraid it's on TV.' Ela watches a smiling *Hard Copy* announcer report on the following story:

'A vaginal parasite was brought into the women's prison today by prostitutes. Police have no idea what it is: there is no FBI file on it, no social security number, they can't even handcuff it properly.'

[TV SCREEN CUTS TO] The jailer interviewed in lipsync:
'*Whores who are trustworthy regulars here, brought it in a sealed shoebox. They said it should be kept off the streets because it was emasculating all the customers and they were losing trade. It even attacked the pimps. It couldn't be shot with a gun as it is an open hole, or hacked up because it moves constantly. A bomb might do it but it'd destroy much else too. It's like the alien in* Liquid Sky.

'*The alien was trapped into a Macy's shoebox by a new girl who'd just come out on the street from Milwaukee. Around 7p.m. she reportedly felt something suck on her um, genitalia. She thought she'd got a bad infection, but it didn't smell fishy; it smelled like old orchids and oxidised apples. She put a mirror in front of it and saw a different layer of labia shining over her own, so she pulled it away even though it hurt a lot, for the alien um, private part wouldn't let go willingly. Her own um, reproductive organ hurt like the thing was glued on it; she tore it off. The kid was bleeding, but you know farm-girls, she even had the presence of mind to put it in her new spike-heel shoebox and tape it shut, before she took it to the elder whores who immediately brought it here, not knowing where else it would be safely removed from their world. I thought they were on crack or something.*'

[TV SCREEN CUTS TO] Two smiling announcers as they amicably discuss:
'*So we know the monster drops its guard and likes to sit on young girls . . .*' '*Perhaps to recharge itself like a dead battery . . .*' '*Aha, very good, Pete. But as soon as a man tries to penetrate it, it strikes fatally. It sounds like those old wives' tales. But it's news, folks!*'

The jailer limply lifts her deepset colourless eyes and opens her skinny arms in a slow-motion gesture of bitter disapproval.

My God, Ela thinks, my cunt has become a female Stanley Kowalski! A meathead! A woman starts to scream from a cell below.

[AFTER THE COMMERCIAL BREAK, TV SCREEN CUTS TO] The jailer, now lipsyncing with a constipated official's concern:
'*I opened the shoebox as due procedure to have the criminal stripped and deloused. There was nothing there. Seriously. It was a big hole, just as the*

women said, and so it was released at once. That is the bare-all truth: "It" is nothing! A signifying absence! The whores begged me to keep it here, promised to sleuth, even pay for its keep. But one has to put away something, in order to keep society calm, so it is useless to imprison nothing. It goes against logic and rules.'

Ela shouts: 'Big? How big? What do you mean by "big"?'

Not big enough to trip over and fall into, the jailer assures her, not like an open well, for instance. Ela: 'Where did she go?'

The jailer: 'That is not a jailer's business. I can send you to the inspector in charge of the investigation. Why are you so interested in Ms Cunt? She seems to me like a loose cannon. The saddest most worrisome part of it is that these types, as you must have noticed, soon show signs of bloat; turn themselves into fruitcakes, like Adjani in *Possession*. I foresee her Moebius-like agility will turn into a trunk. She'll be reduced to fatty tissue. All girth.'

Ela: 'Because I think she is mine.' The unknown woman continues to bellow in the bowels of the jail until her lungs pop loudly like paper bags.

....

Meanwhile, in the same city, at this very moment, her cunt is flooding the world market, oblivious to Ela's predicament.

....

WOMEN'S CENTRAL JAIL PART V
(CONTINUED)

The anorexic jailer: 'Ontologically speaking, there is no such thing as "mine". The liquid around us is a disease. In this liquid all floats loose, nothing belongs to us, not even our bodies and senses. But to drain this liquid is to kill us all.' Ela: 'But now I can't live without her.' Anorexic jailer: 'Life is a homoerotic battle of the bulge. We feed off death to stay alive until all death has been consumed and life and death become interchangeable. That is why I loathe food.'

Ela thinks: When will my cunt learn its lesson and come back? Is this a time of growth for my cunt?

Ela suddenly feels terribly hungry. She runs to the waiting cab.

....

A few hours later, the blaring TV awoke me to the grim reality of my indigestion caused by the fatal large pizza. I blinked at the screen, and, yes, trite as it may sound by now, I was shocked to see:

The cunt was on a talk-show! What degradation! So it wasn't eliminated in the hellish fires of Ray's Pizza! What a waste! Why had I gone so crazy? Was all this worth it? I just lost control . . . How? My eyes glued to the screen, my hand grasping my remote control, I messily spewed out my overflowing nausea . . . into the nearby toilet.

I watched it flirt with Johnny Carson and spread its lips open in front of the camera as if they were legs. My cunt was the new queen of the 'in'! That figured! It was the keeper of the secrets of the 'in'.

I turned up the volume. The image of Ela's cunt filled the monitor! Johnny held it on his desk with the discomfort he exhibits with all the monkeys and other obnoxious pets that visit his show.

But why was 'she' making a fool of herself? Even a severed cunt can have dignity . . . I felt disempowered, and disembowelled . . .

Johnny was asking her who she really was. She leaned back away from him, smiling flattered and mysteriously, tipped her cavity open, and shook with her mute laugh. She was not camera shy.

Johnny informed his audience that she was the latest craze on the East Coast, something like the cabbage-patch dolls (the insult flew by her unnoticed, for being called 'doll' in the past had always brought her good fun). No one knows what she or it is, he said, where she lives, where she has come from; we only know that she can come, he winked, and the audience clapped on cue. We don't know who owns her, who manages her, or how she made her way to the top, but here she is! V for Vulva! The crowd clapped again. V! Viva V!

Johnny said her name had been inspired by her winning streak, her power and mostly her suggestive shape. So the cunt had now acquired its own name and identity! She was a bona fide individual!

V as in Vixen, I thought, Vermin, Viper, Villain, Vomit. Virus, Vicious, Vile Vengeance. Vacuum, Vacuity, Vacancy, Void. Vertex, Voracious Vampire . . . sucking her lifeblood out of countless victims, leaving behind a putrid trail of casualties; including my own recently spilled insides.

Is she a vampire? I wondered. This could explain her power, her magnetism, her sexual hunger, her restlessness, her indestructibility. Vampires had adjusted to the 'sexual revolution' of our times by moving their teeth from mouth to cunt. That's why the encunted Ela had slept in the day, sucked dry her men at night, lived among bones and smells of decay and love, felt neither hatred nor fear, only ennui, and fooled even her mirror, as she had no reflection. Oh, my word!

I'd heard Ela publicly divulge, à la Baudelaire: 'Je suis de mon coeur la vampire.' But I of course took nothing of hers for granted, especially not her words. I had always suspected that Ela's sexuality was a quest. Now I could safely assume that she was searching for the lover who could kill her, whose love would enable her to die after centuries of redundant cities and crowds and long, graceful throats and tired bloodstained teeth. And I was that virginal lover. Was that the self-realisation I have existed for? It had to be done. Now! Now??

'She' comes in and out of the spotlight unpredictably, Johnny told us after the commercial break; she comes and she goes. [APPLAUSE]. But 'she' refuses to be examined by scientists

whose interest has been aroused by this unrecognisable creature, and who are now speculating on the existence on earth of a new, more developed species, Johnny explained. 'If you have any information on V, call the toll-free number flashing on your screens now,' a commentator's voice announced.

Meanwhile, the cunt started to puff, blowing perfect rings of smoke up into the air through her hole. At first I assumed they were the fumes she habitually produced, but the cameras soon zoomed in to the phallic Marlboro stub trapped in her lips. She looked sensual, serene and almost civilised. She sucked on her cig with all her abysmal might and let out the most exquisite fragile airy circles that went up one after the other in parallel layers forming an inverse pagoda like labia sculpted in clouds. Throughout the show, she appeared fascinated by her wetted cigarettes, whose butts she bit out of shape.

Later that night Ela's cunt was also on David Letterman, literally. She was sandwiched between Voluminous Viewer Mail and Larry 'Bud' Melman.

Dave and V had a cigar-smoke-blowing contest which of course she won. He exhaled haphazardly, making nothing recognisable with his smoke, while she blew out smoke-men, smoke-women and smoke-babies, composed of a big ring for the body, a small one for the head, oblong rings for their arms and legs, with little loose hair on the heads, smiling mouths, and dots for eyes and shoes and umbrellas, and with blown-up genitals; they hovered in the air for — David timed it — nine seconds. She was an expert. She had a craft now, a performing gimmick!

Then she leapt on his head and sprawled on it like a glowing toupee. The audience cheered her gall approvingly. She dangled and swung like Tarzan from his nose. She slipped on to his lips, preventing him from speaking, then down to his crotch. The audience chanted: 'V! V!'

David explained that part of her contract for coming on the show was that no one would touch her of their own will. So as *she refused to leave the set, there was nothing to do but let her spend the hour all over David who, being a good sport, revealed a boy's discomfort to get laughs, frolicked with it, made funny wrinkled faces and mispronounced her name, and allowed her to steal the show from his other guests, for the audience did not want to listen to their stories and jokes, busy watching the little clown annoy and arouse the host.*

Who knows what happened after the lights went off and the cameras stopped rolling. Perhaps he had a taste of its foremost talent first hand. Knowing Ela's cunt, I was sure it got what it wanted.

I flicked through the channels and all I saw were ad snipets announcing V's scheduled special appearances on America's Most Wanted, *the resurrected* The Love Boat, Roseanne *and* The Morton Downey Jr Show *where she would match lips with the host: V for Vulgar. Kitty Kelley was writing a V hack-biography for a reported $9 million advance.*

Clad in her wrinkled red dress, Ela sits in the New York Public Library Periodicals Section and skims the day's events in the *New Yorker*. Two announcements give her new hope: Tania Maria sings at the Village Gate tonight, an hour after Jessye Norman performs at the NY Philharmonic. Ela despises the trendy Gate as much as the stuffy Philharmonic, but of all people in the world, those two divine females never fail to send her lawless cunt into the most exquisite ecstasies.

If they sing, she knows it will be there. So Ela is going cunt-fishing again; the day is not over yet. She still hopes.

After her visits to the zoo and the prisons, Ela has now arrived at the city's public mausoleum of surplus information to research the history of other cases of violently emancipated cunts. The impersonal open space conjures up images of a desolate hangar and of her own cold spacious and deserted inner cavity. With uncharacteristic tenacity, she forms a strategy and rises to conduct her desperate search. That's at 8.30p.m.

8.32p.m. She picks a chubby homey albino librarian with tight-clinging thighs to assist her. A polite, melodious, single-breath voice breaks out of her and reverberates through the marble hall, thaws the frigid air, disorients the attentive regulars and inquires: 'My dissertation examines the behaviour of women without genitalia, the lives of women who lost their labia and of the labia themselves. I need information on what happens to their displaced genitals. I must focus on the fate of the dismembered pudendas. Can you help me?'

8.33p.m. The chlorine-blue, red-rimmed, well-read eyes light up, the librarian purses his pale lips and pledges himself to the cause. He silently leads her, like a hospitable mole, through complex corridors to the contents of bulky medical encyclopaedias, immense dictionaries of excisions, abscisions and recisions; treatises about unexplained genital defects, annuals of anatomy, medieval records on women monsters, dusty diaries from macabre operations on peasant women in the Renaissance, reviews of the tortures performed on female servants' genitals by nobles with knives and iron rods, first-hand accounts of South American sexual tortures on female political activists; sexual witchcraft practices, memoirs of pillagers' excesses during well-known and unknown carnages, anthropological diatribes on scarification, purification and fertility rites of extinct tribes, studies of mishandled abortions, archaeological evidence of women's initiation tests from lost civilisations, religious and philosophical theories on the contaminated female genitalia, post-Freudian interpretations of dreamed vaginal stabbings as activated penis envy; until Ela's head throbs painfully and her white-haired, quietly enthusiastic helper, looking like an ant that has been dragging behind it the carcass of a locust for a few days toward the nearest anthill, wobbles unflinchingly into the Sci-Fi section. Ela says: 'No more.' No more text, text, text . . .

9.33p.m. Thus, after having perused dozens of annotated

bibliographies, indexes and tables of contents, Ela has only found that there are no more than nine documented instances of the practice she has come to name 'decuntation' in the history of the world, all found in footnotes. And not one humble word on the fate of the excised genitals; no mention of whether they were fucked, buried, baked, thrown to the dogs, given to the children, made into slingshots, mummified, preserved in salt, used as parchment, sent home as depraved spoils. There are millions of words written about male castration, but not a syllable about a woman who willingly and spontaneously separated from her own cunt.

She wonders if her own decuntation is to be her claim to fame, her reputed fifteen minutes in front of the lens. She tells herself she has a responsibility to write down her own unprecedented story. Write what has never been written before. Break the silence. She scribbles down a working title: 'F/32: CUNTORTED LIFE THROUGH A LENS'.

....

After the Late Night with Letterman *show, which became a classic, the latest craze-cum-sport in the hip-yup circles is smoke-ring blowing. People practise for hours, scratch their throats and burn their lungs trying to create the simplest designs, a smoke-fish or a smoke-baby, but most are still puffing up tiny balloons at weekly smokathons. Contests are held on every other campus and nightclub, but no one can recreate V's artistry or break V's Guinness world record.*

Now V has her own TV show: Puff That Pussy *(c). Every week she can be seen blowing smoke-valleys with smoke-trees and smoke-sunsets and smoke-picketfence houses. V is the champion, the idol, the star.*

Her fans are organising clubs, and collecting any merchandise with her image on it. V fans get together on weekends to blow smoke and exchange memorabilia, stories and addresses of people who have seen V in person. PTA groups vote her their honorary president and fly her to remote areas of the country to give a live demonstration of her talent. She goes, blows, but lets no one touch her. Dark rumours of sexual perversions suddenly rampant, break out when she leaves town.

PS: Darker tabloid rumours are daily killing V off: V is dying of AIDS in a provincial hospital, they assure. Once a week a doctor appears on prime-time news to reassure V maniacs and V watchdogs that she is in perfect health. The next day the gory stories resurface.

PPS: I worry that one of these days they may be true; and then a clever mechanical rubber fascimile of Ela's cunt will appear puffing away on the monitor, while Ela's special cunt will be rotting away in quarantine. The big companies won't let such a money-making trend go.

For V is omnipresent. She performs televised live shows in Vegas, smoking in the open-mouthed pose that is the V logo shot; lasers kazoom as V goes up the clouds (painted stairs) in a laser tunnel, cheating her own fog machine, glowing artificially like a seasoned star. See V in a red-white-and-blue bolero. V in a rhinestone Elvisoid suit. V advertising Coors Light, Orion, Amex, Pepsi, Nike, The Heart Association, The Olympic Games, Wrigleys' Circus. V is the message of the day. V is the media queen. V is the other half of TV.

Even TV Guide is publishing a special section called V Guide. V is on the cover of every self-respecting magazine. The reason:

V is the new reincarnation of the American identity. V has found her own voice and broken away from the bondage of an abused childhood. V rose out of the claustrophobic hereditary prison that was her selfish single parent: the human body. Now that V is free, every American wishes they had as much guts as V. V is the star-spangled emblem of the American ideal of individuation: any American can make pots of money. Me. Myself. I. V is living proof. V is the new role model.

....

Ela walks home from the library, to avoid being stormed by subway passengers and cab-drivers. The humid dusk is buried in car exhaust.

To her discomfort, Ela runs into a lover – K.? the masterpiece – she had some years ago, whom she vaguely remembers she had promised to marry but left town nauseated hours before the ceremony, as was her habit with planned weddings. K.: 'How are you?' He looks down at her with his shy, slothful eyes and she assumes he speaks to her cunt. His gaze is frighteningly deep, like a well in which she throws a stone, waits to hear it hit the bottom and when she gives up hours later, she hears a faint sound of stone touching stone. It is the gaze of a sleepwalker, who can calmly watch a lion tear a child to pieces. He wears a white Comme Des Garçons shirt, a black stretch miniskirt, long thick black Guess tights and shoes, an exquisite gold vest designed by Lacroix and a red Kanzai Yamamoto cape. He reminds her of her old self. It no longer shocks her to recognise a face that is not her own.

He says: 'Time doesn't heal. You left me with a bleeding ulcer. You left me with an erection?'

He reminisces about the *Butterfly Remote-Control Clitoral Stimulator* Ela used to wear which he loved to operate, by sitting on the other end of a classroom or office or family dinner table, pushing the red button, and watching her jolt, writhe, moan, sigh, scream and come in front of the perplexed spectators. Ela waves goodbye. But K., like all men, considers nostalgia a turn-on: 'I miss your cunt. I'll wait for it as long as it takes. I know how much it's worth. I know it now more than ever before!'

Ela feels like an impostor. She doesn't tell K. that it is gone, kaput, that she misses it too. She says: 'I think every cunt is low in calories.' But the shock value of her line sounds fake in her ears. Looking at K., she suddenly realises she has become an adult.

As K. looks at Ela, he recounts how transparent she always was, his old agony that she would turn into smoke and disappear and elude him, his fear that she would crack like glass, as they were walking hand in hand, and how he kept wondering how such a creature could exist and how the world had suddenly become so beautiful, how Ela could light up the universe. A flush glows through her white cheeks, like crimson flames through a thin sheet of ice. Her aloof, pliant face holds the nonchalance of an actress accustomed to public stares.

Ela: 'Solitude is sentimental: it prolongs the handshakes, it loves nostalgia, it imagines that the awe of being next to another being is universally felt. It scares me.' She thinks: I am no longer I.

K.: 'I will always be in you.' He used to shout that when he came, it was his battle cry. She starts to leave again.

K.: 'I am hearing Ela speak, oh my God, I stand here listening to Ela! If I don't watch myself, I'll do something silly. I spent the last three years getting ready to be able to copulate with you, correctly I mean, and I feel I can do it now,' K. discharges and smiles indolently as Narcissus, while his exquisite fingers make indecent designs on the lenses that he, being a photographer, always carries on his shoulder, gesturing like a boy who stands around patiently waiting for the adults to finish talking about grown-up subjects and notice him.

Ela has left. Her past is an eclipse; she has only the present, her need to begin the book *f/32*, and the image of her confused cunt that pelts her mind like an endlessly repeated urban-angst MTV clip.

....

THIS TOWN AIN'T BIG ENOUGH FOR THE THREE OF US

On my TV, my link to the real world these days, I watch an MTV game show giving out V prizes, but I can't keep up with the hurried voice over: 'V 3-D Arts hologram watches, V earrings and pendants, V scarabs, V candleholders, V skilfully laid in leather or silver . . . etc.' going by at nine frames per second . . . too fast for me . . . Click!

I switch channels: the President addresses the nation. He says: 'All over America, Operation V is under way and it's a winner!'

Click! Fuck this remote control . . . Read my lips: No more cunt!

I have a laughing fit, for I can just picture Ela when she first sees her cunt's image on a US-made product: let's say she drops into that store she likes, Manic Panic and recognises her cunt smirking on a watch. She goes mad: where is her goddamn cunt? What has it done to itself? Who has this much access to it? This will be a deeper wound.

And she still won't even remotely realise the dimensions of the international consumption of her cunt. She'll think her cunt has been used, or abused, by artists whose work is exploited by

CONCERT PART II (CONTINUED)

Leaving K., Ela runs home to change for the night. But her mind is not on her looks. She's thinking about her research. She turns on the TV looking for some pop-culture inspiration for *f/32*, and, lo and behold, there is a documentary on the story of a penis on PBS.

What, Ela asks, is the dead, amputated penis of a native Australian doing in the Pitts Rivers museum in Oxford? David Attenborough, Abdul Tee-Jay and the other enthusiasts on the programme fail to make that clear. This 1890 penis is only remarkable for having become detached from its owner and travelled across the world for no apparent reason.

The PBS special celebrates the fact that the penis, now in rigor mortis, after a century of being exhibited in the book shops, salons and colleges of Oxford in a jar of formaldehyde, is going back to Australia to be ritually buried. I can top that, Ela tells herself.

Merde, Ela now thinks. Should I've put formaldehyde in that jar instead of plain water? Has my baby cunt rotted and turned maggoty because of my scientific ineptitude? Why didn't I watch TV earlier on?

She decides to tour natural history museums and classrooms in search of her cunt. What mischief would the amputated penis and her cunt embark upon if trapped in the same jar in a museum cupboard! Enough to change the course of human evolution beyond recognition.

She considers the evidence: the modern fascination with body horror movies (e.g., *The Hand, The Creeping Flesh, The Mummy, The*

Skull), and the New Age fixation on Aboriginal mating can make *f/32* a blockbuster. They can also ruin her runaway cunt. She switches to the movie channel HBO:

Steve Martin stars in *The Man With Two Brains*, a love affair between pickled and unpickled matter. This is the closest to real love Ela herself has known: in her body, between mind and cunt. Now. Everything seems to fit her new situation.

She makes rough notes: Maybe *f/32* is really a story of love; of confused love, to be sure, a love so personal it can never be finished. A love story so true that it will finally kill the author.

Ela pledges to write it with both her mind and her cunt.

....

Old retired couples in trailer parks all over the country, black adolescent mothers rapping with headphones on their ears, ex-marines and ex-athletes travelling by train and bus across the States back and forth, upper-middle-class businessmen playing putt-putt golf on the weekends in the suburbs, nurses, neo-Nazis, nerds, neurologists, nereids, the needy, all wear atrocious V-shirts with V's silver wet likeness exposed proudly and mindlessly on their chests these days. They are ubiquitous.

No, they do not see it for what it is. They don't revel in the nastiness, they see it like a trendy new Wheel of Fortune.

I wonder: Would they like their own genitals advertised on every paper, on sale in every supermarket, stuck into the mouth of every toddler as a teething aid, thrown to any house pet as a sucking rubber toy, worn by every Joe on the street, massively reproduced, sold below cost in big closing-down sales where the crowds run to buy three for the price of one?

It's not another hot commodity, damn it, it's Ela's and my cunt!

Famous designer B. Blass is buying copyrights to the V mould to manufacture V-Blass paperweights. Chef Fontainebleu at L'Odéon is bargaining for the exclusive right to feature his new nouvelle cuisine delicacy: V con escargot. The Japanese are training their chefs to remove the poison safely and prepare V sushi instead of toro; TV hosts are already making jokes about the US President throwing up on V.

P. Picasso is bidding for rights to use V's shape for her new handbag collection. S. Spielberg is looking for a script about extraterrestrial procreation, a sci-fi porno, that will be starring V.

V is the biggest trend ever: the Western world is bombarded by V posters, V coffee mugs, V notepads and pens, V hats, V ties, V sheets and towels, V cigarettes and cigars, V perfume, V lollipops, V Oreos, V gum, V chips, V lunchboxes, V make-up, V cameras, V calendars, V blenders, V grinders, V choppers, V rockets, V ovens, V juicers, V kites, V condoms, V furniture, V cars, V planes, V hot-air balloons, V cartoons, V storybooks with titles like V **Takes the Kremlin,** *and of course loads of V underwear. Even Pynchon's book,* **V,** *although unrelated, tops the bestseller lists. And V is given honorary PhDs every week.*

In the dunes, the heart of the land, V is the most familiar image since Jackie O. became a widow. A super-speed rollercoaster is being built in Disneyworld inspired by V's famous 'curvacious triangle', painted pink and named V's Ride of Terror. A new skyscraper is being erected in Paris and designed by I.M. Pei as his interpretation of V, to be named **V la France.** *The competition is cut-throat.*

Countless industrious Americans are capitalising on Ela's cunt and rolling in big dough. Any smalltime local merchant or hard-thinking tycoon can safely invest in V these days. Except for me.

....

CONCERT PART III (CONTINUED)

Ela looks at the mirror all around her and feels that slowly, unknowingly, month after month, she has been crossing the mirror's borders. She feels she now belongs to another world. She doesn't know where. She can't touch herself any more. She can't remember coming. She is lighter. She doesn't need the mirror. She feels beyond.

She throws on a Mae-West-as-Delilah gown: silver, tight, endless, a beam of light. She writes a postcard to her parents: 'It's not easy to picture black when you wear it. Maybe I've been sitting on the wrong grave. All day I form my first and only word: "Come" in my mouth, so when the moment comes, I can too.' It has a picture of Gala nude, holding on to an elaborately moustached 8-shaped mirror.

She drops it off in a mailbox and hails a cab. The cabbie is a Nepalese wife importer who drives a cab on the side; by the time he gives her a brochure and enumerates his possessions from the Park Avenue penthouse to his Frère Jacques jingle car alarm in order to seduce her, they have arrived at the Philarmonic; he doesn't accept money of course.

At the entrance a snobbish herd is milling around, looking each other up and down like adversaries, flaunting clothes, thin bodies, escorts, terrors, smiles, accents. The well-coiffed heads turn to her: is it an ascension? Is she going up or coming down? Seeing them, Ela thinks: Isn't it comical that I should wear a dress and take food and need a cunt? I am a trick performed for company. She gets seated. Wrapped in yards of crisp red satin, the dark diva comes.

On the first note, Ela floats into a heaven of contentment, of grateful inebriety. Her eyes close, her ears open to the marvel, her body is drenched by the ineffable. She gasps for air. She comes.

Jessye Norman looks directly at Ela's closed eyes. Ela feels J. N.'s eyes leave indelible prints on her lids as if an archetypal woman were extinguishing her cigarettes on them. Ela wonders: Does she know what unbearable pleasure she gives? Does she understand I am consumed by her? Is she aware of her tremendous power to heal, to exorcise?

Ela mutely calls: Singe me, smoulder me, swallow me, in your dark ardent female mass, unroll for me the fuming passion of your vastness, the enormity of your flesh, of that torrid gushing throat, don't stop!

For the first time in six months, Ela feels a transcendence.

It is her scintillating cunt that comes to Ela. Ela doesn't notice the culprit jolting about in her resplendent lap, and the audience can't distinguish her brilliant cunt any more than they can see the shape of one crystal in the heavy chandelier of the ceiling. The hedonistic cunt instinctively seeks Ela at the time of its heightened pleasure as it enters wave upon wave of orgasm, jolted about as if hit by electric current. As if the magical voice comes from inside it.

Ela feels whole and calm, and attributes it to the music.

At the end, both women pant and drip with sweat. For an instant that won't end, Ela opens her glinting eyes and they pour themselves into one another, lost in the perfect hyperbole that is the other. Ela and J.N exchange souls.

The overheated cunt lies unconscious on Ela's silver lap like a tumbler who has performed a fatal cartwheel. The wanted cunt is knocked out within arm's reach, but Ela doesn't grab it.

If Ela lowered her cleansed eyes now, if she were not suspended absolutely still, her thighs would trap it and with one simple swift move, she could repossess it. Wasn't that her purpose?

Instead, they lie together like kittens basking in the sun. Ela offers the world her best smile. All three for a moment are in love.

When she comes to, the Siren is bowing and Ela gets up to leave. Love exists only for fleeting seconds, Ela knows. She must not look with her everyday eyes at the Beloved, speak to her, scrutinise her, feel her skin, her wrinkles, her exhaustion. It's her Orphean task to abandon J.N in time.

As she makes her way out in the midst of the applause, Ela feels her own slippery marvel slung from her belt and swinging to and fro. So why am I possessive of this cunt? she asks. I wasn't possessive of it when I had it. Let it live free. I know I can't look at my Beloved.

The gay cunt slithers and tickles her as it comes down, like a child on a slide. When Ela reaches the kerb, she has second thoughts.

But the cunt has disappeared, faded to black.

....

[SCREEN FADE UP TO]
SWIFTY and the CEO lecturing on V:

SWIFTY: 'A creature beyond the average man's comprehension. V has a flair for publicity and audiences. It arouses her to be seen. But that is also her greatest defence: when aroused, she secretes some kind of silver liquid that wraps her like a cocoon and makes her slippery, impossible to grasp and difficult to see. She also emits a temporary fog on occasion that also obstructs her from the viewer's study.

CEO: 'V exhibits some sort of memory and critical faculty: she carefully avoids those who seem eager to imprison her and does not go near anything resembling a machine or a scientific instrument, which could scan her; with the exception of cameras. She is too intelligent to be a form of proto-life. She belongs to an evolved type of meta-life. No other creatures from her planet have yet appeared, with concrete proof, on our world. This makes her hard to study for we don't see her interact with her own kind. So far, her only instincts are for exposure, performance and freedom. She does not sleep, rest or hibernate. No one knows yet what she subsists on . . .'

I watched the two experts on the news discuss the V-personality. I learned nothing new about the cunt, but admired how far human imagination could reach. A confirmation that, even under such dire circumstances, deeply soothed me. Those inventions of the mind were the only benign effects of the V epidemic. I enjoyed the merciless battles conducted nationwide

*among headstrong scientists over the true nature of my cunt,
the theories sprouting up like poisonous mushrooms out of the
brains of closeted monomaniacs hungry for recognition.*

....

THAT DEAR ELUSIVE ALIEN:
BEAUTY OR BEAST?

Based on the assumption that we know only one-third of the
underwater life in the Amazon River, naturalists led by Egbert von
Fuck, are convinced that this wonderfully wet creature we now call
V is in fact the legendary *elhinidia amazonon*, the pink-spotted silver
riverbed slug known in antiquity from the works of Hesiod.

Wendell Carp, a subway conductor and bimonthly angler,
disagrees. He identifies it beyond doubt as a Mississippi River
leech that has caused death to hundreds of his fishing colleagues
over the years, a species he has found on occasion in his black
rubber gumboots.

Dr (Miss) Phing Pon-Tse, a part-time filmmaker and full-
time exploress, claims to have photographic evidence of this
breed of the Venus flytrap from her extensive research in the
Indonesian jungles.

Dr Ramanugan Bhopla ascertains that it is the evolutionary form
of carrion turtles – *trionyc gangeticus* and *lissemys punctata granosa* –
that were introduced into the holy Ganges at Benares to feed on
the countless corpses deposited in the polluted river every day,
and clean away the continuous procession of rotting flesh floating
downstream.

Pearl-oozing sweet-tasting squid – kalamari – of the kind
appearing live these days on US TV, has been studied in length
at the Papadopoulos marine lab in Piraeus, whose researchers claim
that the V species was stolen from their live specimen lab by Arab
terrorists.

Unidentified sources claim that the Dalai Lama has recognised

V as the original incarnation of the Buddha's third eye. 'If you touch it, does it not weep?' the Dalai has reportedly said. 'It weeps over the misery of human existence in the First Path of the Kalliyuga era.'

CONCERT PART IV (CONTINUED)

....

I feel gloomy and confused in the cab. I think: The streetlight and the buildings are beating against one another, as I remember the bare feet of monks beat, when they crowded frantically by the parlour window at dawn to watch the bare-chested sailor boys, looking like tiny violins exploding in the air, and like thin trees whitewashed up to the waist and from the waist up like bronze sardines galloping inside a fishermen's net, disembark with a comical smell of premature lemons; and at that instant it was obvious to everyone present that a lot had ended, and so the photographers and the murderers gathered their liquids and their tools and left town for good . . .

There is another passenger sharing the cab; a shaky Filipino boy feigning an Ivy League accent: 'I asked the driver to stop. I am grateful for the chance to look at you up close. What are you made of?' I: 'Dreams. Light is a spasm.' The cabbie comes from Jordan, studies computers in Queens, has a girlfriend from Java who cooks good Chinese food and thinks I am a movie star. He wants to kiss me. He asks for my autograph. At every traffic light, he unrolls his window and calls out to the other cabbies: 'I got a movie star in the car! Follow me down to see her come out. She is unreal, man! I got a dream!'

The Filipino: 'One last question. Is there life out of the rainbow?' Myself: 'In spring, I like the orgiastic creatures that elude and recede before me. In winter, I like the taste of boys for breakfast, the sausages of their tongues, the jam of their lips, the hot pancakes of their hearts, and the creamy milk from their cocks.'

The Filipino gets off with me on Bleecker. I enter the Village Gate. I feign the attitude of someone present. I think: A nightmare is nothing exotic. Human relations are collisions of nightmares.

A sleezy mafia-handsome wrinkle-free Jewish Moroccan film and lit. agent in an Armani suit, geometric haircut and rings on his fingers, introduces himself smiling his white teeth, gives me his business card, a typed list of his clients, his current shooting projects and publishing deals. His sentences become a monotonous hum in the background, a private elegy that reminds me of men talking to me as I fall into post-cum stupor. He squints at me as if he is looking straight into the sun and says: 'I want to fuck every woman alive!' Me: 'Start with my grandmother who at ninety-six is low on offers, for after the first few thousand women there won't be much of you left or she may die, so here is her number.' My breathless voice spreads out like molasses.

Ashamed of his unappreciated pickup, the Moroccan looks to the men on other tables and bitches: 'Feminist! I knew her eyes would open like flying saucers when I said that line.' In fact my blinding eyes roam the busy basement like searchlights: is the cunt here yet?

This time, I warn myself, I have to shut off the angel's mouth and hold on to my cunt if it comes. I think: Too many vanquished cocks have been rinsed away from between my legs like ripe rats who scurry through the city sewers; in the meantime, the ice inside me expands.

Tania Maria comes on stage in a loose, long housewife blouse covering her abundant thighs, short black stretch pants and stiletto heels, and attacks the piano. Her eyes are torches. I revel in T.M.'s dark, greedy, cruel, volcanic, monkeylike, gypsy's face, her powerful protruding teeth, her bony ankles going up and down like a locust's, her hourglass body that I must relish naked.

T.M. woos, coos and calls in new vowels and rushing spontaneous meaningless words. T.M.'s reckless, beguiling, unpredictable scat vibrates through me from toes to hair, and gives me goose flesh, tears, spasms, orgasms, blackouts.

The crowd watches the Brazilian maenade motionlessly as if she were a TV screen.

I think: She will devour me, in a single preverbal gulp, this is true language, I feel it in my groin, I want that uncontrollable voracious voice inside me to mingle with my tears, digestive fluids and cum.

My cunt comes on my tin round table, vaulting, pining, twisting, overwhelmed, thrown in exalted rapture. It froths and oozes like a disturbed earthworm and drips gooey stains of saliva. No one notices it twirl in the cognac glasses and on the mouths of the beer bottles.

I look at T.M.'s teeth, and ask: Take me, take me. I see T.M. as an immense inflated breast, a single backside cheek of sea that rises before my eyes blocking all vision, lulling me, prodding me on. I am happy here.

When everything is over, my cunt lies sprawled on the sand floor, gaping upturned and phosphorescent in the fake moonlight. I look away to avoid the suddenly aged T.M.'s glare, and I see it. But again I've forgotten why I am persecuting it, what I could ever want from this poor exhausted epicure. As from one seasoned Quixote to another, I wink at it. I feel bloated, pregnant with love; or something worse.

....

Ela thinks: As things turned out it would be easier for me if I had given it a name. I could now call to it without feeling ludicrous. How can I express it: 'My cunt, my cunt, why did you forsake me?'

Ela knew many men who had names for their cocks. They would say: 'Romeo is on the balcony', 'Ronnie is making a statement',

'Tiger is roaring', 'Marco Polo is on', 'Let the Pope give you blessing and so on'.

Ela saw them as unnecessary metaphors and looked down on these attempts to humanise or exorcise instincts. Now she sees that it can be useful and comforting on occasion.

Her Mom's vagina is called Penelope. Ela grew up hearing Mom complain: 'He goes straight for Penelope, you know the type', or 'In this bikini half of Penelope is showing'; Mom referred to Dad's cock as Ulysses.

Mom did have a quiet, unobtrusive, faithful Penelope between her legs, a content, chubby fluff. Ela's cunt was too nervous, stubborn and argumentative to grow fat like a eunuch. She knew early on, that there could be no name for it, no 'nice, civilised way of referring to it', as Mom advised her to do. It was a nameless elemental urge, a mythical female. So Ela thought when she was in its grip, at its beck and call. Now it seems harmless, easy to look at like those cosmeticised, patched up vagina photos in *Hustler*.

....

Nothing is working: I can't kill her, and I can't become her. And yet she is mine. Ela is mine, the cunt is mine, I am mine . . .

The last time I looked in the mirror, the reflection that I saw was mockingly unfamiliar to me. It was a strange, frightening image. Or rather a disembodied smirk. It made me want to get out of my skin.

Have I always been separate and apart from the rest of creation?

I only know that I do not recognise myself. The old illusion of 'I' has died and rotted away and no new one is replacing it. All the bonds that held me intact have been broken because of that. And I pour my last hope like crystalline cum, drop by drop, down the parched throat of this improbably aged reflection of a demiurge. I can't even be Ela, I've failed.

I am now experiencing the uncanny realisation that my

*reflection has become stronger than me and I have become like
an image in the mirror . . . I can no longer remain alone in the
room with my reflection. I fear that if I try to turn away, she
will come after me. We are two beasts face to face, hair risen,
preparing to do battle.*

*All those loving hours spent in sweet contemplation are lost
for ever! And with them my soul. I say to myself: Death . . .*

My lips are closed, yet I am afraid of my own voice.

*I fear to go out and search blindly for that impossible object,
turned subject, that has kept us together. I move like a man on
a death mission. I've heard it said too often that once a mirror
breaks, it can never be glued together again. Yet I have no other
recourse but to persuade myself that there is hope.*

CONCERT PART V (CONTINUED)

Outside in the street, the world is full of scurrying extras.

The overzealous Moroccan offers to drive Ela home. She is still
in a daze. He leads her to a tall curvaceous swanky silver Silver
Cloud Rolls, immaculately clean and glowing. She slides in: it's the
perfect fit! He shuts the passenger door with a low, comforting
thud, as if he fears waking someone up. She is a sculpted piece of
radiant silver superbly displayed within another steel work of art.
He turns on the ignition and reminds himself to drive in a relaxed,
stately, centred attitude following the whim of the Cloud. She lets
the watery purr of the sublime engine soothe her nerves, the sound
of gathering forces pacify her raw heart. He wants to be seen at this
moment by everyone he's ever known and secretly devises ways to
show her off to the world. She doesn't feel human, but an extension
of the double-gauge nickel and chrome plated flawless bodywork
that contains her. He has the fanatical stricken eyes of a sensitive
executioner, and he is not stingy with his smile. She rests back,
feeling loved.

He turns on the radio: '*L'amour est un oiseau rebelle* . . .' with Julia Migenes and Placido Domingo. She thinks that this would be a better world free of tension and war, if everyone were issued a Rolls. He thinks that every Rolls should come equipped with an effigy of Ela dressed in silver sitting serenely in it. She is surprised that his one gentle step on the anti-lock brakes at the red light can so effortlessly stop two and a half rolling tons. He runs his dark hand through his glossy backcombed hair and steals febrile glances at her, making sure she is still there. She notices that the visor mirror distorts every reflection and that makes perfect sense to her. He sucks on the thin metal arms of his Dior sunglasses suggestively because he feels he can do anything to her. She wants to run the big air-conditioned car out on the beach, get it stuck deep in the sand and wait for the tide to come in through the windows and submerge her.

He offers her champagne from the polished oak cocktail cabinet and chilled oysters from the brass fridge under his armrest. She would rather fill the vehicle with champagne and bathe in it, sailing through town. He shows her the jar of Gray Poupon he keeps alone in the lovingly veneered, spotless passenger cabinet. She wants to live inside this strong smooth womblike dome from now on, as in an invisible travelling cocoon. His dark skin shines like expensive polished leather. She wants to carry the car comfortably, weightlessly and protectively coiled around her body at all times like a snail's shell.

He fidgets a lot. She wants to masturbate. He wants to have her at any price. She wants to make it come. He says: 'The happiest day of my life will be when I wake up one morning and realise I have fallen out of love with you.' She says: 'Some people like to have sex while looking in the mirror. I find that to be excessive. I think one mirror is enough.' He invites her to a literary party. After some negotiation, she sells him the rights to her first book, *f/32*.

At her doorstep, he holds the door, rigid in his open long grey shoulderpadded coat like a uniformed chauffeur. The invisible loudspeakers boom: '*Les voici, voici la quadrille des torreros . . .*' She glances back into the cavelike mouth of the roaring body, and wonders: Does this sickly recognition I have just felt, prove that I myself am an object?

But from her upstairs window, the car looks insignificant.

She doesn't recognise the effulgent wet eyes that meet hers in the mirror. She conserves her senses for one purpose: to understand. She rubs her temples, shuts her eyes and begins to think:

....

Once, a lone blind snail slowly crawled out of V on screen, on a children's show. It turned its nervous antennae this way and that, carrying its heavy spherical home on its back, and looked intent on going God knew where. It was unaware that it had just crossed out of the circle of the world's most wanted cunt, it had efficiently and moistly penetrated the world's tightest and first emancipated cunt. It showed no pleasure. I realised then, to my mirth, that the record was broken, that her power was waning, for this was the first living being to go into Ela's cunt and come out unharmed and unaffected. And in the solitude of my bathtub, I cheered the little champion.

....

How badly does Ela want her cunt back? Why is she unable to want it enough to go out and get it? Why did she not take it by force when she had the chance? Is this quest over already, or what?

She thinks: So other people can get close to it, but I am kept at a distance. I, who carried it for twenty-one years and kept it happy no matter what the cost and how much it disgusted me; because I had to feed it, like keeping a pet boa, having to throw live mice into its mouth, hearing their desperate squeals and its grunts of bliss as it swallowed them whole and spat out seconds later the leftovers, their juices still dripping out of it; I, who adjusted to its savagery, because I felt I was part of it; after I gave up my life for it, after I spent my youth tending to it like a thorny garden, the beast refused to grow up. After I grew used to it, and in some ways even identified myself with it, how am I expected to feel now that it denies me? We were after all united in flesh, not in metaphor, and I became who I am because of our union. I didn't abandon it in a gutter, it had no reason to leave, all I wanted was to have a better look at it.

So how can I not feel betrayed and deserted now? It puzzles me to see that porcupine take off to conquer the world leaving me, the one who was supposedly in charge, leaving me gaping. I am not trained to take in this reality, to accept it and live with it.

Ela squats, opens her thighs, closes her eyes, opens them and looks at the wrong place – her mouth, not her vagina – and on reflex jumps back, even though she has seen nothing frightening, loses her balance, falls hard on her ass and shouts: 'Ouch!' She hates speaking aloud when she is alone; it makes her feel needy; it wounds her ears.

Ela feels that without a cunt she will close off and retreat into the dreams that take place in her head. And why not? Does she owe it to the world to be part of it? No. As it turns out, her cunt was her main link to the outside world, her cunt was her opening into the world. Now she is finally free as she always dreamed of being free as a child. Why search for it then? Now, immediately, she can go to the empty family house on the deserted beach and live alone off the land, among the flowers, the cacti, the fruit trees; she can swim, fish, and sit alone for ever after thinking up stories to please herself.

But first she must write that *f/32* book and get it off her chest.

···

I think: Now the cunt belongs to me alone. Ela is no longer
claiming it, she's given up, she's fallen into the old American

trap. She's ready to exploit her sufferings, go public, become a celebrity, write a bestseller.

Now Ela wants to teach her cunt and this country a lesson. To call the sucker publicly by its name and publish her old f/32 photos that show V as a white severed fly sensuously sprawled out on unsuspecting persons. As proof that Ela knew V long before it became famous.

As its owner, Ela can receive a chunky percentage of the profits from all the V offshoot and no longer feel robbed of her cunt. If she has to live staring into it wherever she goes, the least it must do for the years she nourished it is to acknowledge their old connection.

Ela will outshine her cunt. Her cunt's power and talent is in fucking; unless it can exploit that in public, and with the public, it will be a passing curiosity. Ela, meanwhile, can become V's translator and biographer, V's Voice. She can go on talk shows to tell her story. She can speak at length about the pain of women who lose their cunts. Oprah will break into tears and admit there was a time in her difficult childhood when she herself, albeit for a short fortnight, had been abandoned by her malicious beefy vagina. Housewives will call on live shows to confess the loss of their vaginas. For the first time, thousands of women will come out with the shocking truth. Countless cuntless women will pour out their hearts! People will realise that their genitals are by this point in history quite separate from them and science should make them optional, portable, transferable, disposable, only to be worn for sex like lingerie or edible gel.

Ela will be admired for her honesty. She'll socialise with the Hollywood brats, talk to B. Walters for an hour about her insecurities, pose in Playboy semi-nude, visit the White House and Third World countries, marry a few times, attend charity galas and buy houses on both coasts. She will be a pillar of the world. She will never make up with her treacherous cunt. That is where I will step in.

I am freed of the responsibility of writing this book. Ela can plagiarise me. In exchange, she will leave me her one and only cunt. And this quest.

....

Ela thinks: I will go off by the sea and live on fish till I die. So what? There are people born without a cunt. I used it a lot for a while, had the experience. It's better than letting a doctor cut off bits of my ass to reassemble for me a funny-looking new cunt.

She decides to call overseas for family support. Mom picks up:

Ela: 'Hi, I feel I am not a woman.' Mom, a sculpture of white marble on the receiver, replies: 'Baby, how tedious, why?' Mom lingers softly on each syllable as if she has to think to remember the next sound in every word. Ela: 'Something is missing.' Mommie: 'Of course, honey, there is always something missing, that's how things are: parts of them are missing! The world is full of missing parts.' Ela: 'It's not that; it is like I am missing.' Mommie: 'Don't do a thing! Don't think! Rest, take a bath, get a facial, go on a cruise, wax your legs, and don't have sex!' Ela: 'I have done all that.' Mommie: 'Sex is exhausting, darling, it's a lot of hard work. Take a nap by the mirror.' Ela: 'I've ripped my skin away with my own hands.' Mommie: 'You need a nice dermabrasion, a deep peeling.' Ela: 'I feel I don't have a womb.' Mommie: 'That's not so bad. You can adopt. And get X-rays. Lay your skin on that metal.' Ela: 'But it's true!' Mommie: 'Darling, truth is a lower-class notion.' Ela: 'If you were here, you'd see for yourself.' Mommie: 'I'll take a little trip, we can go shop for silk.' Ela: 'No. I like missing you. Bye.'

Her face in the mirror shows no sign of the self-flagellating component within her prodigious endowment of self-belief. Only in her eyes can one gauge the toll of the wearing oscillation from solitary resolve to rapturous hopelessness. She thinks: This panic keeps me young. She thinks: I've always been beautiful when I've been able to look at myself as if watching a distant fire. Then she leaves.

....

I feel nausea again. I run to the toilet and vomit. I am sick of being sick. I think: I will wear a sign: PROUD TO BE ILL.

I am now in a silver concoction of space-age punk boots, taffeta dress in the shape of a spiral orchid, a cobra-shaped hat worn in memory of my departed cunt, and on my way to the party at the Writers' Café. I can't be alone with my decisions and my TV any more. Despite my rustling clothes, I run the ten blocks in order to kill my fear.

An immense Yul Brynner-like doorman lets me in with an obedient canine smile, without asking for invitation and ID. I feel taken for granted: Is seeing believing? The beast thinks I am making eyes at him.

He has the eyes of a werewolf. I slide inside through his arms.

The rooms are thronged with people dressed in black and silver.

....

PARTY PART I

At the Writers' Café, Ela looks around: only one small vision in pink – pink leather skirt, pink leather jacket and beret, pink fishnet shirt and stockings, pink suede pumps, pink messy hair – stands out in the back among the crowd. She thinks: Crowds used to be so enjoyable. I miss the crowds that used to gather on the docks: the foreign mouths, the blinding reflections on the army coat buttons, children chased peacocks, tin wastebaskets rolled, drums called, splendidly detached lithe dumb wombs were on sale, limping lepers begged 'Please deprive me of my wounds', hundreds of cats in heat wailed as if they were children being butchered by Herod, and merged with the racing sirens that couldn't catch up with all the fires, until the first sunlight stabbed the tourists in the wide eyes.

....

PARTY PART II (CONTINUED)

A man in thick-rimmed glasses and a silver tie who looks like Allen Ginsberg spits in my mouth: 'Cut that sexy stuff out! If you keep it up, I'll have to go out and solicit, like a martyr.' Simultaneously, a ghostly white-wigged inarticulate male in a Freddy Kruger outfit, Andy Warhol's double, exhales in a gossipy voice: 'What do you think of men? I need an honest informed opinion.' Within the minute, a third thin bespectacled young man, dressed in a paper silver suit stuffed at the crotch with noisy newspaper dramatically bulging, maybe Keith Haring's ghost addresses me gloomily: 'We aren't well because we don't fuck.' I: 'Mom warned me to eat men like fish. Until you develop the immunity of the locals, you can get hepatitis from seafood.'

Warhol's spook whispers in my ear: 'Mmm, I. Whom would you try?'

Why did I come? Going to parties is a form of suicide. That is why.

A fat-bellied old man, his bulk swaddled in a silver paisley-leaf kimono, who may be N. Mailer, with childish eyes and undefinable consonants, slurps a double martini, fingers a long cross-eyed Czechoslovakian model, and tells me confidentially: 'American anti-intellectualism is a CIA plot. The CIA invented AIDS, the floods in Bangladesh, the market crash, and modelling.' Andy's phantom rasps: 'Huh, how many men here have you tried personally?' Keith: 'Night cruising is dead.' Ginsberg announces: 'It's my time to strip, jump into the vodka punch and howl. Are you coming?' A chinless man with brows like thunder-clouds and a chicken's neck, sniffs me with the indignant sternness of a tortoise testing unfriendly air and says: 'The dailiness, the dailiness. The deception. The plight of the Male Jewish Novelist!' P. Roth?

A chorus of partiers chimes: 'Who doesn't have AIDS in this room? Raise your hand!' I: 'I must make a confession. My cunt is a razor. When I masturbate, you see, it's messy.' Chorus-leader: 'Attention! This is a film set. A screening will follow. Don't wander off!'

I have come here to lose myself. Lose my self. Which self?

A man with haggard day-glo skin, insomniac eyes, a floor-length silver mink and a black umbrella, looking like G. Vidal: 'The roar of the deluge outside is deafening. We'll have to run into the sea to find refuge. The North won't survive. The intellectuals will die; only the fishermen will swim on. If our bodies can't adapt to the sea, grow fins, scales and so on, there will be no humans left.' Roth: 'In these outpourings of hilarious angst and lyrical befuddlement, lies a story that's probably apocryphal, since all stories are apocryphal.'

Private security bodybuilders stand outside the bathroom and allow one person in at a time. Brawls and stripteases start. Waiters in drag are flying on to the carpet, asses up. My eyes search the crowd for someone not reduced to chaos by the mere effort of living.

....

PARTY PART III (CONTINUED)

Ela is intrigued by the fanciful pink girl smothered under a heap of flushed men on the couch. She cuts decisively through the packed rooms, reaches her, sees the girl's smile and stops dead. Then she pulls out her party invitation and studies the silver smile printed above the words: MARCH 21ST COMING OUT PARTY: COME FIND OUT WHOSE.

It is the same familiar smirk. Now that the smile appears in front of her, in a shroud of steam, she recognises it with terror. Is it possible? It is the typical grimace of her cunt, which she'd seen often in the mirror, then later on the pavement and in the jar. If nothing else, Ela still knows her cunt when she sees it. No?

The oversized asymmetrical labia are here, in the smile, these are not mouth-lips, the tiny hard clitoris in the place of a tongue. Can it be a coincidence? Are there more cunts like hers wandering and smiling around free? Ela decides to embarrass herself if she must.

Ela bends down towards the pink creature until her silver face nearly touches it, and whispers: 'Excuse me . . .' Her voice is an intimate, breathless tickle that travels under the skin and into the blood. She calls: 'Come.' This, she thinks, it will recognise.

The cunt puckers its lips until they wrinkle. Ela: 'I don't know how to put it, but, you must surely agree, we know each other from far back. How do you get along without me? For my part, I've tried abstinence, but the thought of it, knowing I can't fuck, eats at me.' The cunt keeps its lips pursed and nods solicitously. White steam evaporates from its pores, enveloping it and Ela's face in a silver Felliniesque cloud. Ela: 'What have they done to you? You look pale. Is anyone taking care of you?' The cunt looks diffident, like a child being reprimanded. Now Ela is certain: the intoxicating scent – which was Ela's – of hot wet sugar with lemon and old orchids rises under her nose. Ela: 'What better position could you have asked for, you had your independence, I never believed you escaped of your own volition. Is it possible that you wanted more attention?' She wonders: Why doesn't it run away? Is it willing to come back?

....

PARTY PART IV (CONTINUED)

I look around the steamy, infested dungeon until I come to realise who is heating up this abominable bash. I see the hostess sitting on a gold throne, gleefully overseeing the orgy. She is dressed in pink Victorian garb from head to toe. I see in her eyes the gleam of a knife. With the instinct of a hound, I attack her.

The cunt retracts into its pink clothes like a snail's horns in its shell. Inquisitive hands land on my bending ass.

I hear Mailer shout: 'Let us go into the sea. Do you know boats of madmen were sent off into the ocean with provisions to stay away from shore and die at sea? It was a sane practice for centuries.' Roth buzzes like a mosquito over my ear: 'This is the dread that emanates from the most commonplace appurtenances of the world of utter stupidity. Take my advice, buddy. Avoid The Breast *or* The Nose *or* The Metamorphosis. *Concentrate on* The Unnameable . . .

I reach out my hand, but the cunt slides down into its clothes. My fingers follow it through the fishnet shirt, down the leather skirt into the stockings. Somewhere there I lose it.

I rip the tiny translucent weblike threads of cum that hold it in the garments, and come out the bottom empty-handed. I search the floor, crawling under the couch. There is a crowd of moving feet on the rug. I shout: 'Open up, my cunt just escaped again!' 'Sorry, I lost my cunt!' 'Move out of the way, my cunt's run off!' 'Someone catch my cunt!' I can't overcome the absurdity. High heels step on my hand.

Ginsberg falls on his belly but he doesn't help me; instead, he confesses to me: 'Earth is a sexual globe, a rotating stage upon which organic scum act out countless continual scenes whose content is wholly sexual. The colours, smells and sounds of all life have evolved as sexual attractants to keep a trillion romantic plots on this planet moving. The maker of this sexual drama or farce is female . . .'

Throughout all this, writers are licking my ears, sucking my neck, biting my hair, twisting her nipple, pinching her ass, each concentrating on a single area, as if they are following an earlier plan.

Still on all fours, I am being raided by comments from every

direction: 'Is V your relative?' 'V-day!' 'A déjà-Vu!' 'Vim!'
'Ventriloquist.' 'Vanity!' 'Prince's ex?' 'Vesuvius!' 'Verboten.'
'Variable.' 'Vice, Virtue, Vibration, Vessel, Verve, Vault, Vapour!'
'Veto.' 'Valentine!' 'Visionary!' 'Vulcan?' 'Voyager.' 'Vogue.'
'Vernal.' 'Vis-à-vis what?' 'Voltage.' 'Victual!' Viva Voce.

In the throes of this terrible confusion, I whisper to the world
one concise last command: 'Shut up!'

··

PARTY PART V (CONTINUED)

This time, Ela knows better. This time I will speak, she determines,
I've no curiosity left for these public games at being free. All these
recurring setups or memories are too predictable.

She is not distressed that her cunt has disappeared in the crowd.
It's understandable. She is not surprised that it has achieved such
social prestige. It always had. And as she looks at the curious
writers that have gathered around her cunt's abandoned clothes,
she no longer feels herself the onlooker. She feels inside her the
wisdom of a leader.

'I have no glands,' Ela bellows at the crowd, 'no guts, no follicles,
no cum. The moisture on my flesh is dew. I am a planet in orbit, I
perform my rounds unconsciously.' The uniformed doorman hovers
over her protectively, like a hunchbacked retard perched on the
belfry of Notre Dame. She is standing on the gold couch. Her eyes
look as if a spatter of sun and sea came between her eyelids.

The crowd expands. Ela calls to her audience: 'Close your
eyes.' They feel their legs grow heavy and uncertain as if they
were stepping on to a stage. The partiers obey with a sense of
accomplishment and relief.

The crowd, now with closed eyes, hears her whisper: 'Let go.
Love the way your body moves.' They all feel she is their priestess
who can relax them into perfect meditation until they wake up
as new beings. Is she that sex guru who travels around the world

performing cleansing spiritual public rituals for free? Some join their hands in prayer. Most devotees move rhythmically in trance, like people at a reggae concert. 'Exhale. Open. Breathless. Great. You're full of light.' Ela sings.

The believers hear her breathe near them, in them, as if through individual earphones. They visualise sea waves and sighing mermaids. They lose themselves fast.

'I touch your golden third eye. Feel me. Relinquish. Easy. Lie down.' She thinks: This is the message and the essence of *f/32*.

The crowded auditors lie on their backs on the floor and all the way out on the pavement outside the café, their eyes stay closed, their lips parted, their limbs loose, their hearts at ease. They abandon themselves to the higher, better being, eager to soar into new sexual awareness. They remind Ela of overturned powerless insects.

They lie stretched out below her, moving slowly and erotically up and down on their buttocks. They glow. Ela remembers standing on a school veranda watching her classmates stretch and exercise on the hot school yard at dead noon, as she now hovers above the crowd, watching this massive democratic midnight masturbation conducted in her honour.

Her voice echoes through the bodies more sincere than anything they've heard, like their own inner voice of knowledge: 'I am forever exposed before an anonymous Other. There're always two kinds of people: those who watch and those who feel they are being watched. I have carried myself as a huge aesthetic burden of unfathomable implications and readings. Now I propose a third way of living: free from the mirror.'

This is the power of language, Ela thinks. And the power of sex.

Once it was my dream, she remembers with astonishment, to die coming on the busiest avenue of the world, stormed by people of all ages and creeds touching me irreverently: I would be immense; and that initial infectious touch would awaken them, jolt them into revolution: while I would come, the people would rebel and change the world. My death-orgasm would end all fear, faith or sacrifice. But I don't want to be exalted, sexually or otherwise. I don't need any more chains.

Ela shrieks her muezzin orgasm call. The crowd sees the face of God. And as the doorman ejaculates over the couch, Ela slides out of his watch and runs swiftly away, apparently undetected.

....

DEAR ELA: SOMEBODY UP HERE IS WATCHING OVER YOU

I realise that I won't survive unless I keep writing. I must write Ela's destiny before she writes mine. Is it too late for words?

[SOUND EFFECT: A.P. EMERGENCY BROADCAST]
'From the head office in Intercourse. Penn. At this very moment, V freaks are working the phones, organising surging new waves of V Awareness, letting the country know about today's guest appearance of V's owner whose coming out tell-all autobiography marks her as America's new pop philosopher and sage.'

....

Ela goes home and lights the fire. She listens to Stravinsky's *Firebird*, crouches next to the mirror and hears a growl in her stomach: what makes her think it is worth anything to stay alive? Where does she think she is going? Why does she keep going? She thinks: I am not even a woman who bites her nails. The firelight flares in her eyes, and they flare in the mirror. She is stunned by the unworldly flower-like youth that looks back at her, animated with pleasure like a bright girl on a roller coaster. She resembles her cunt. A thought blazes through her mind: Am I my cunt? Am I my own lost cunt? The fire blazes up. Ela wants to jump in it.

....

*I think: We die for words over and over, why not die
for a cunt?*

....

The phone rings in her closet. Ela hears her recorded voice on
the answering machine, whisper as if in breathless panic: '*Go away,
keep quiet, don't make a noise, leave me alone.*' After the beep, her
Dad tells the answering machine: 'Ela, will you let me come? In
my visions you are giving birth and your vagina slips out instead
of a baby and it is crying, so I swaddle it. I don't know what to
feed it. It is pestering me. I am losing weight. What can I do? It's
so cute. Why can't I just come and hug my own daughter?'

Ela thinks: Did my cunt throw that party? Where does it
live? How can it live? Who would believe this? Is it time to
pinch myself?

....

OUT OF CUNTROL

*Cuntsucking marks have been identified on the corpses of 900
victims so far. The killercunts come into crowded city areas and
allegedly toss themselves at helpless men. They give no warning:
no yelps or grunts are heard. The sound of flesh being sucked
and ripped is the first sign the pedestrians have that they are
being attacked.*

*We quote the testimony of a rare survivor: 'They rammed me
against the trees in the (Central) park, I gasped, but I kicked
and flung (the cunts) off my genitals, I knew that if I went
down I faced a prolonged tormenting ending, I yelled my lungs
off. I felt my life being taken from me drop by drop, chunk by
chunk, trapped in the mouth of a crazed life beyond all appeal
or humanity. It was worse than rape.'*

These events have caused worldwide shock. Sympathetic heads of state expressed their deep concern to the Mayor of New York. International men's groups are dispatching squads of men to replenish the declining male population of the city. But even such volunteers are decreasing as the deadly sexual assaults receive more coverage.

The new plague has replaced AIDS as the major public concern, since cunt assault is today the number-one killer of men in New York. AIDS seems harmless in comparison and has already faded from public memory; for, as some die-hard gay-rights activists have pointed out, 'these cunts are much more democratic in their distribution of death'.

....

Ela walks through a leafless, charred forest under a clouded sky. A terribly old, mummified man, with a white beard down to his feet, approaches her. He trips on his hair and asks officially: 'Where are you heading?' Ela recognises him as the decunter.

Ela [continues to walk]: 'Where I've always headed, of course.'

A huge black tree falls with a massive 'thump' on her chest and face, flattening her on the ground under its impossible weight. She can't breathe. Painfully she crawls out from underneath the jagged branches, bleeding from her unsightly wounds. At her first step, the nearest tree falls on her body again, crushing her, ripping her thighs and pushing her deep into the rocky ground. The same procedure follows. As soon as she disentangles her torn body and rises, she is thrown back under another falling tree. She doesn't seem fazed. For, throughout this eternity, she knows exactly where she is going.

She is certain that she will never go back where she came from.

....

A CUNTAMINATED CUNTRY

The entire nation is alarmed. Men feel endangered in their homes and in the company of other men. This has caused panic among workers in such male-dominated industries as auto plants and the docks who are in the high-risk category. Many of them failed to report to work this week. Men refuse to go anywhere unaccompanied by women, as women have been respected and unharmed by the 'beasts'. Dozens of bachelors have committed suicide in fear of a more horrendous end awaiting them.

Yesterday at 9.20 a.m. a man in Long Island allegedly saw his male-dominated household raided by the killercunts and two of his sons murdered.

According to what the anonymous Long Island victim, 52, a divorcé, told the reporters from his hospital bed, he was having breakfast on Monday at 9 a.m., when out of nowhere an army of little pink creatures broke in through the doors and windows and swooped down at his crotch.

Despite the pain, the victim, a National Rifle Association member, managed to grab his gun from a drawer with them hanging on to his flesh, and shoot at them. It was impossible to aim well as they were terribly small and agile. One of the bullets landed in the man's thigh, but he didn't know it until later, for the pull at his genitals was much more intense. He was saved by his sons, who just then walked into the kitchen. The killercunts dispersed to attack the boys and he fled to a neighbour's. The unfortunate father had nine sons, of whom two were dead on the spot and the remaining seven lie in critical condition in the hospital.

When the troops finally arrived, the killercunts realised they would be outnumbered and took off. But the soldiers felt defeated. 'I can't imagine what we'll do when they start hitting schools or monasteries!' a sergeant told reporters. 'I'll never forget the physical humiliation as long as I live! No man is safe on this earth any more!' the tragic father cried as he was taken away for plastic surgery.

Ela wakes up from her dream-infested nap. Does she miss me? Ela wonders, lying awake in her round bed. I made her life easier, I made it simple for her to get whom and what she craved. I had the language, I kept up the appearances, played by the rules and secured her prey. Isn't she having trouble, with her overt ways, finding mates? Does she like to be misinterpreted, to be taken for the wrong thing?

Ela is torn between two forces of equal and opposite gravity, so she can only stay still. She can give in neither to her desire to live in total isolation, nor to her urge to jump into the thick of things and change the world. She used to give in to her cunt, which at least followed one singleminded direction and kept her busy, so she did not have to choose either extreme. That is why now she can neither abandon her footloose cunt to its fate and live happily alone, nor come out into the glare of the world to demand what is hers.

DEADLY CUNTDOWN

Daily reports of more wild-running cunts coming into NY are alarming city officials. Experts claim that the runaway cunts had been repressed. So they emancipated themselves and began to hunt in packs. They are multiplying to dangerous numbers.

It is impossible to calculate how much havoc they have already caused, for many of the assaults go unreported. The killercunts mostly attack men in remote suburbs and seedy areas of the city. They 'rage and rave and rant and raise the devil', residents report. All city ambulance services and emergency rooms are on 24-hour standby.

No killercunts have been apprehended as yet. Police hounds, specially trained squads, guerrilla forces and the National Guard have pooled their resources and are hunting for them round the clock, but so far the police's only success has been to save the lives of partly devoured victims, after being called by neighbours who heard cries.

The police are distributing artists' stretches of the 'beasts' based on survivors' descriptions. They are the only pictures of them available, but the cunts do not look half as menacing as they are alleged to be. Until we know more about this menace, there is no hope.

Psychiatrists and sex specialists have offered their services to help understand the 'killer's motives' and interpret the killercunts' instincts. No pattern of the killers' preferences has emerged, however, other than gender. They attack anywhere, any male.

There is no precedent for such unbridled sexual violence. City officials have declared a state of emergency in NYC. If the city shuts down, including such nerve centres as Wall Street, the country and the rest of the world will feel the blow. Suggestions of moving business headquarters to Washington are made but the manpower required and the costs involved for such an undertaking render it impracticable.

Lunch hour protest marches are being held in NY and candlelight vigils are taking place. Gun sales are skyrocketing. Churches are overcrowded and priests work overtime to meet demands. Group memorial services are now available. The victim toll has reached the 9,000 mark.

Men fear to travel alone and go out only accompanied by police escorts and bodyguards. These precautions, however, have not reduced the number of men found dead in ditches and side roads every morning. Experts fear that, in a population as large and diversified as NY's, the cunt crisis may prove impossible to contain for some time. Killercunts are definitely mankind's new and possibly greatest scourge.

'Only I, the loneliest creature, know the answers. I hold the answer to the violence and to the confusion at the tip of my pen. I can explain the chaos and dispel justice. I can have V arrested for inciting unrest and countless murders. I know that this bloodshed is taking place for a cunt's fun. This truth cuts me inside and often I bleed. But I, the mirror, am the new Kassandra. I can't tell why. But I am never believed and never revealed . . .'

I only know that there can be no words that don't refer to Ela's cunt. This cunt is all-inclusive. It is an ingenious unprecedented dictatorship.

I must remember that words are my tools, my tricks.

In her dark loft, in the light of a match as she lights a cigarette, Ela sees her face in the mirror and it is new: it is suddenly devoid of greed. Her lips that used to crave orchid-smelling cum look harmless as a fresh open strawberry, no longer pale, but bright red. The sweet, putrid smell of love that always rose out of her loft has been replaced by cool clear air. Her ears, usually so tense and sensitive to sounds, look relaxed like seashells. Her body that had become a coffin for spent men feels young and new again.

NO DISCUNTENTED WOMEN

Who are these women whose cunts are wreaking havoc? This is the question everyone has been asking of late. Why haven't they come out in public? Where are the bodies that initially hosted all the dissatisfied cunts? If the reasons for the killercunts' greed were established, many believe their lust could be controlled. Yet, despite the authorities' guarantees of anonymity and free psychiatric help, NY women have been indifferent to pleas for their cooperation.

Meanwhile, as women are safe from the terror and walk the streets freely at any time, men have taken to dressing up as women to protect their lives, with reportedly positive results. These antics seem to work well enough to lead the city's social agencies to advertise the practice. At the same time, tests are conducted nationwide for the discovery of an antidote to the killercunt deadly bite.

So far there is proof that using women's antiperspirants can multiply a man's chances for survival. Such products are now greatly in demand. It is not known whether the killercunts have the sense of vision, but it is certain that they identify their victims by smell. This explains why the majority of deaths have occured among physical labourers, joggers, dancers, athletes, gigolos and generally men who had been sweating or sexually active. The official advice to every man is: Stay feminine, cool and celibate and go out only in the company of women. Women, of course, have nothing to fear.

....

Right before dawn, the phone rings in her closet again. Ela jolts. No one but her parents is supposed to know that she has a phone.

An anonymous dark voice breathes heavily into her answering machine: 'I have what you want!' Ela runs and grasps the receiver eagerly and holds her stomach in her other hand carefully, as if handling a sharp blade.

The following is being recorded on her answering tape:

Ela: 'Where?' X: 'Are you well? You sound stuffed up.' Ela: 'Is she there with you?' X: 'For me there can be no other, "she".' Ela: 'What do you want, to hand her over? Name your price.' X: 'You've always been Dad's little girl and Mom's little girl. It's time to change.' Ela: 'Are these your demands?' X: 'You want to be my little girl?' Ela: 'Are you blackmailing me?' X: 'People seduce people to tell them what to do, isn't that your motto? Follow it.' Ela: 'Is she all right?' X: 'When I couldn't have you, it hurt like hell.' Ela: 'When did all that happen? Who are you?' X: 'I thought everything out. You can have it, without the rest of me! Get your wish, Ela!' Ela: 'Where is it?' X: 'I have it wrapped in a dinner napkin right here in my lap! But it's bleeding badly. I cut it off with my Swiss Army knife.' Ela: 'You cut it! Again?' X: 'Didn't feel a thing. It's my homage to you.' Ela: 'Stay where you are. Don't move, don't call anyone, don't touch any more knives. I'll be there in a minute. What's the address?' X: 'It is my Votive offering to you! When you come, you'll have my very real living cock to take home with you! I know how much you need a cock these days, so I've cut mine off to give you.' At that, Ela hangs up, nauseated.

She thinks: America is hopelessly sick. I need a bath.

....

THIS ONE GOES OUT TO THE ONE I LOVE

Now I know what took me ages to admit: language has been invented solely to sustain and expand the myth of love which keeps us well-behaved and blind. I have tried to behave like a wild animal or like a superior, ultra-refined creature, but for one who has been taught to understand words, there is no escape from the trappings of love.

....

THE AGE OF WOMANIPULATION

Experts are warning the public now against the subliminal messages hidden deep inside V's form. Their own message is: Don't look!

Professor Olegario Casagemas has written five books entitled, The Age of Manipulation, Part I, II, III, IV, and now V. He accuses the American ad industry of camouflaging sexual images in hundreds of commercials and TV programmes. He claims that V is nothing but a ploy to boost sales of various products. He alleges that it is a creation — not unlike Frankenstein's — that comes out of an amoral consortium of big company labs keen to destroy their competitors; the corporate villains include Estée Lauder, Du Pont, Pfizer, and even NASA.

By 'embedding' pictures of erections in the model's face in an ad for Malboro cigarettes, for instance, Casagemas claims manufacturers and advertisers trigger a Pavlovian connection between their product and sex. Casagemas, an ex-marketing man, distinguishes an upright penis hidden in a bottle of Tanqueray gin, and labia woven into the frosting of a Betty Crocker cake-mix ad. 'This,' he says, 'promises to moisten the housewife's vagina. It's all in my latest book.'

The American Advertising Association has taken to attacking Casagemas with a series of ads ridiculing his alarms. One of these shows a Scotch on the rocks with the copyline, 'People Have Been Trying To Find Breasts In These Ice Cubes Since 1957'. The latest AAA ads show V on satin sheets like those used in the memorable Marilyn Monroe calendar photos, with the copyline: 'Some People Claim To See Female Genitals On These Sheets Even Now'.

But experts are agitated. 'I'd feel uneasy about this sort of ad,' says British psychologist Jock Burnham, who uses subliminal 'flash frames' in personality tests he carries out for recruitment companies. 'Repetitive flashes have been shown to influence mood. A single flash affects a susceptible person. Millions of children could be affected. This barrage of V imagery is a global security risk.'

Yet as news of the brainwashing reaches the public, it serves to popularise V further. In the home of the hard sell, people clamour to watch V on TV and theatre screens in order to try and depict the sex.

'TV networks have strict rules about using subliminal frames in adverts or regular programming,' a network spokesman said. 'V's shows have been run in slow motion but no hidden frames have been found.'

....

At dawn, Ela sees the pink daylight (the colour and blinding brightness of her cunt) suddenly attack the window panes and the mirror.

Mechanical noises, aroused birds and crowds and the bright light assault her all at once. She closes the shutters and takes a bath.

In three hours it will be a day since she woke up with the knowledge that she would be reunited with her cunt. She should have asked the mirror before trusting her intuition, but these days it has been looking empty and spent. It hasn't been present lately. In fact, it hasn't been itself for months. It offers Ela no safety and no insight any longer. It is lost to her.

She listens to Callas singing 'J'ai perdu mon Eurydice . . .' as she dissolves into the bathtub and now she understands Eurydice's last lines (according to Browning): 'and all terror defied, no past is mine, no future: look at me!'

....

There is no such thing as a rebel without cause. Look at me!

....

Ela covers herself from hair to ankles with a black-*diamanté* gauze punctured with tiny silver moons, under which her pores give out an unreal light. She wears red Russian boots and feels like a sturdy peasant. She takes big steps and chooses: I won't look for my cunt ever again. All ambition is vulgar. It is so embarrassing to want something. I have made my peace. Today I will move to another town. No, to a seashore.

It is a cool grey morning and the streets are full of trim constipated men in running shorts and windbreakers who lope breathlessly around every corner with massive sweaty dogs on leashes. Their blind energy turns Ela off. She walks, lost in thought, dragging an immense silk pink laundry bag behind her to the neighbourhood laundromat.

On the way she passes the Mary Boone Gallery. A sign outside reads: LIFE IMITATES ART. The trendy art inside is always so flashy, boisterous and funny that Ela habitually strolls through the gallery on her way to do the wash. So she now glimpses through the glass-window, hoping for an eyeful of kitsch. Then she freezes.

....

The two adversaries exchange the blank, fierce glares of prey startling hunter, hunter startling prey. She runs in, in a blind fit. Her opponent waits for her, frozen, exposed on a gleaming oval shield. They're looking each other in the – blind – eye, as if they have been eternally pitted against one another. The tension cuts ice.

....

Ela drops her bag and walks into the gallery. She can no longer think coherently about this affair. A wail is piercing her insides.

She shouts: 'Are you following me? Leave me fucking alone!

A pert early-riser photographer, looking like he is made of vanilla-flavoured frozen yoghurt, interferes: 'Excuse me Miss, would you mind? I have permission to photograph this piece! I'm due next door a minute ago.' Ela ignores him: 'Show-off. Go on Broadway. Act the sap. But leave me out of it, I want no part of it. Don't try to get *me* to believe this identity crisis, this sacrifice bullshit. I feel no guilt. I am the one in pain.'

The cunt snarls at her, tied as it is to its mirror-made stand.

The still-photographer, now looking strawberry-flavoured: 'The curator is out, I have a job to do, and how am I expected to deal with all the freaks who walk in here?' Ela: 'I thought you were the freest babe in the world. But I was just a foil!' The photographer, from under the weight of straps, tripods, cameras, films and shooting schedules: 'Are you the model? I used to be a model myself. I may be a simple social climber, but I only fall for European women. Can I shoot you?'

The cunt is spinning, bloating condescendingly under its artistic and elaborate chains.

Ela: 'Ungrateful cunt!' She really wants to say: Come back.

The photographer turns *chocolat* and stammers: 'Miss, you turn up in every picture! Try to stand more to the left and give your speech. Bend your head backwards and shake that silver fountain of hair!'

· ·

The stagestruck opponents take in the might and madness of the other, quickly glance behind them, inhale, hold their breath, and unleash their love, charging through the thin glass of the gallery at full blast.

But can they act? Together? What are they trying to communicate?

· ·

The rebel cunt looses wind under the yolky yellow light, wearing Maria Sneider's touching pout from *The Last Tango*. It is the centrepiece of an op-art exhibit titled THE SECOND COMING.

It is a performance piece, judging from the muscular naked mulatto who hangs from the wall behind it. All his anatomic details are eclipsed by his cock painted silver to match the crucified cunt. He too seems nailed on the wall by his hands and feet. He reminds Ela of a Da Vinci drawing. His eyes bleed, but it could be red paint. His mouth is taped shut with white tape. He is alive, for his chest rises and falls with each breath. The crucified man, probably the artist, is restfully asleep.

All is calm. Around him hangs a drip-painted jungle of masks, teeth, newspapers, condoms, huge gowns, broken TVs, stereos, cameras and pink confetti. One stereo plays a Verdi aria sung by Jessye Norman.

And in the centre of the room, on top of a tall crystal stand, alone on an oval mirror lies the frivolous cunt, tied daintily with cobwebs down to the mirror, pretending to be an object crucified. The symbolism can be cut with a knife.

....

It lies on the mirror and — apparently in direct response to what Ela asks at that specific instant — rolls over, jolts, yawns, sulks, flips, pants or pouts. It slides back and forth, absorbed in something like thought.

This is the first time it seems to pay attention to any words addressed to it. It looks sincerely affected. It changes colour from silver to deep scarlet red. It bends down and looks (?) at its own reflection.

....

Ela asks her cunt: 'Is this the paralogism of love? Is it joy that overflows from me like an ocean?' In her cunt, a metamorphosis takes shape. The labia fold themselves, and from within the unseen vortex emerges a single glistening tear like dew. Her cunt is crying.

Ela confesses to her cunt: 'I am learning to approach something outside of myself and incorporate it. Or is it the reverse? I am learning to stand back from something inside myself and examine it for the first time. I am becoming see-through. Does it show?'

The cunt drips. Tears well up in its labia. It is too painful to watch. Ela: 'It seems we would know it if we belonged somewhere, for instance you between my legs, not out in the open. But we don't. We refuse to belong. We have no home.' She speaks as if she is singing a lullaby. The dewy cunt is looking up at Ela. Ela: 'Do you deny that you are after all a cunt and an important part of me?' The cunt makes no sign of denial. Ela: 'We're misfits.' The cunt nods.

....

I am once again the felicitous observer of an unprecedented, gratifying, perfectly executed spectacle. In all my years — has it been only years? — as their loyal voyeur, I have never seen either one of them so animated, so real. Never before has either one confronted a person, or each other, or themselves, with such conviction.

....

The cunt with a determined effort breaks its webs and pops off the mirror, leaving behind a wet, sparkling circle of steam. It throws itself with a high backflip at Ela's moving lips. For a split second, Ela is so stunned that she almost swallows it. The syllables stop midway in her throat crammed together in a jam. She is choking. They kiss.

....

I see that I have been deceived. This is a simple moral fable. I mistook it for something else entirely, a roman policier *or a comedy of manners. I basically was kept in the dark as to what direction this adventure was going to take: an operetta, a straight drama? It has been none of the above. I expected to cut into Gordian knots . . . to fulfil age old prophecies and prayers . . . to be the referee, as Ela's cunt would destroy her mind and vice versa. I expected a death in the end . . .*

f/32 is nothing other than a map. A rudimentary map charting the inaccessible terrain of the inner workings of a woman's lust, in mind and in cunt. A ride.

....

In that heartwarming moment, Ela takes out her tongue and licks her little burning cunt, pulling it gently into the warm enclave of her mouth; not as a bullfrog catches its prey, nor as a cat bathes its kitten, but simply as if she were licking a dry corner of her lips.

It occurs to her that she can swallow it now in no time.

The cunt is back inside her where it belongs. Her body can conduct the trial and distribute its own justice: either by digesting and then excreting the cunt or by reinstating it in its old position.

She closes her lips. This gives it a taste of its own poison: an awareness of what it is, of how it feels to those inside it, what it does to others. The cunt has its first real look in a mirror.

It does not fight for its life, but slithers swiftly deeper into the smooth, moist, tight interior. It likes being there. In itself.

....

Suddenly the mirrors crash with a roar. Glass shatters everywhere into numerous sharp pinpoints of stars, staging a breath-
taking show of light, a towering exhibition of force, a gorgeous
explosion of rainbows. The glass windows, frames, display stands
and walls crumble like a crystal toy palace. Shards of every shape
and size from the hardly visible grains that nestle deep into the
skin to the monstrous guillotines that fall from the air, pour *en
masse* over Ela and her now protected cunt. Something is gone
amok, Ela thinks, unmoved.

There is a frenzied discharge, a lovesick paroxysm. Ela feels it
personally directed at her. It is nothing as simple as an earthquake,
or a silver foaming ocean. It is a desperate expression of fury.

Something is in hysterics, she repeats to herself. What?

Hi. It's me. Your old pal. Your own fucking mirror. Remember?

Ela feels her cunt in her mouth like the leap of a heart.

Its taste reminds Ela of a semi-liquid fruit that she has eaten
in India called *targola*: a semi-transparent, imperfectly round, very
smooth, fragile fruit with juice in the middle that is fragrant and
mildly sweet like fresh coconut water and spurts out suddenly when
one bites into the soft flesh, leaving a milky, thick, oily aftertaste.
She has to summon all her self-control to stop her teeth from giving
in to their instinct and biting through the core of her cunt.

In Ela's mouth, her cunt bends right and left shyly like a child
who deserves a spanking but will be forgiven because it is doted
on. It taps on Ela's tongue to test the consistency; it wraps around
it to tense the muscle, embraces it, and sensuously glides further
into the crimson recesses of her mouth that is waiting, holding
its breath.

Ela's tongue does the same thing: it traces her cunt, testing its power, resilience, flexibility, at the same time and in the same way that her cunt becomes familiar with her. Both feel pleased.

....

It does not please me that the cunt has returned of its own free will. I feel used. I should have led Ela to her cunt I, the consistent one. What else was my purpose here? Am I the failed intimacy? Both blind and invisible?

My eyes have nothing more to show. So I poke them out. For, as was once true for Oedipus, there is nothing left for me to see. I possess no memory of my own and no self to be remembered by. I am suddenly shattered. And I am discarded like any other old, cracked and cloudy mirror.

....

Ela bravely confronts this assault. She stands under the heavy rain of tinkling glass falling into a sad heap of shards on the floor. She feels excited both by the proximity of her cunt and by the unmitigated spasm that takes place outside her. She bleeds where she is cut by the falling shards. She laughs, caught in the beauty of her own throbbing blood. She looks into the blast and peals away in genuine laughter.

All around her hundreds of sparks and specks dance in the crisp air. As she stands in the heart of that spewing volcano, that uncontrollable consuming blow-up, that jagged Armageddon, she senses the cut-throat orgasm around her: the grand finale.

Then the great white-hot breath quells. Dead? Asleep? Fulfilled?

She looks around. Both the artist and the photographer lie under broken mirrors. The photographer's camera has stopped clicking.

At the end of this majestic show, Ela cannot help herself: she gives its maker a standing ovation.

The world stands still, even devout.

People all around the world hear Ela whisper: 'I love you.'
They don't know that she is speaking to her cunt.

The cunt, with a few slippery backflips, drops out of Ela's mouth and attaches itself like a slug on Ela's pubic mound on top of the gauze that covers her. It hangs preposterously, like a damsel holding on to King Kong. Ela touches it lovingly, as she might touch a lover's hand as they walk side by side in the street. She smiles in a new, unfamiliar way: a mute deep joy, too big for her lips, pushes from behind her huge eyes, almost causing them to burst.

Thus Ela leaves the gallery taking quick, small, ginger steps, with her sparkling cunt hanging on to her black-*diamanté* gauze from the exact spot where it once hid under her clothes and inside her skin. Only now it is publicly and proudly carried.

From the ruins of glass rises a dense cold fog. Ela walks out of this swollen wave of misery, as in a biblical episode where all life unites into one solid shattered mass, as at the end of a long journey.

Only, here, the world that Ela knows has just broken itself.

What has defeated me? My mouth has fallen off, my fingers, my crystal irises. I've been dismembered as Orpheus was by maenades, except that my attackers are uninterested in me, and I fear that I myself make this happen. What will become of my files, my research, my book? Who was I? What have I learned? The last illusion is disillusion.

The undead creatures that come to steal the blood of the living, and change shape in the dark, have won. They are creatures of their own imagination. I fought against hope. As do the brave.

The cunt slides down under Ela's gauze, looking for security in the familiar. It reaches her lower cavity. It warps itself into it, and feels how on every surface, it fits so perfectly. Slowly as a snail, it proceeds further into the crimson recesses that are its lifeline. It cuddles her. She cuddles it. Both feel loved.

Distracted from its regular daily chores, the world stares dumbfounded into an immense superimposed screen composed of silver steam that suddenly hovers and flickers in front of the buildings, the sky, the fields, the objects of the world, encompassing yet hiding in stage fog, all existence. Ela's mirroring face, which looms before them so large, transfixes the people. They look at the screen and do not realise: These two strange new creatures are us. They don't see themselves. Sucked into the suspense, the terror and the magnitude of the moment on screen, victims of their own eyes like those privileged to see Medusa, these vacuous lonely people are blessed and yet doomed, from now on, to do nothing but absorb in bliss the popular imagery that is creating a new landscape on the shallow atmospheric big screen.

Ela does not feel the eyes of the world turned on her.

For her cunt that was lost to her has now come back. The rest of her body does not sag, but joins the celebration and every nerve feels the purifying pleasure that the cunt causes in her soul. Her scalp tingles, her fingertips caress the air like tentacles, her limbs bubble, her spine shivers. The words that had been locked in her throat blow out in a slow, endless exhale, almost a wind, which empties her insides until she is an airless cavern. But her soul is full.

A giant Ela floats, lost in herself, on the celestial screen. The world cannot touch her as she hovers complacently in the sky.

She walks washed in the mists. Feeling the cool breeze blowing through her as through tree leaves, Ela has a silent private orgasm.

The sensation is beyond dreaming. Ela cannot think at all.

*Once upon a time the mirror looked in the mirror and desired a fusion. But, gazing into itself, it saw a blank gap. So then it gazed into the Other, and it shattered. The world has lacked a firm support and a deep root ever since. (**A modern epitaph**.)*

WHY SHE FOUND IT

(ELA'S AUTOBIOGRAPHICAL NOTES, TENTATIVELY TITLED: F/32)

In the beginning of all there was the mirror, on every side, wide open. The mirror created everything. I first opened my eyes (or was it, its eyes?) while going through the mirror; or coming through the mirror: from my mirror view, this and the other side were identical.

The mirror taught me how to talk, walk, defecate. I dressed up for it, smiled into it, wore the 'fuck me' look on my face to please it. I discovered myself in the mirror: something outside of me was myself. I was always in the picture. I existed by excluding myself. My otherness was clear. And I could see behind my back.

Since then, I slept with the mirror or woke up to it. I went into it at impossible mirror times or came out of it at impossible mirror places. Living through the mirror was not a sequence, an addition, a story. I said mirror words. *My breasts had a mirror smell. My words mirrored my mouth. My smell mirrored my breasts.*

I had mirror feelings. Great fatal passions were impossible in the mirror. Glass breaks from too much love or hate or anger. So I could not be held. In the mirror, la dolce vita *lasted for ever.*

Though I looked as if I didn't care about anything, I held on to my hiding place: the mirror. The mirror was not a closed erect system. It was a river. When I looked into it for over a second, I no longer recognised myself. I never focused. I was exempt from volume.

So I lived in continuous orgasm. The mirror invented foreplay and afterplay. It prolonged sex. The mirror was the source of all suspense. It could not obey. It was inconsistent. It was a revenge. A zero. Like looking into the firing squad, or into the lens.

My reflection looked at me, not at herself. The image of me didn't see what I saw. It saw what I could not see. Both my presence and my absence were announced. Each side wanted to taste the heart (the death) of the other. If I moved too close, it (or I) would float away (or drown). The mirror, like a camera, froze my eyes.

My eyes were self-contained: convex mirrors. Men desired me (or their reflection) to acknowledge (devastate) them. Men saw the mirror as real. So they lived out of place. There the mirror looked like a window. Men desired the evil eye: the gap between my flesh and my eyes. Men said: 'I want to know what you are thinking.' But living in the mirror was a continuous rehearsal. I felt no loss. What I saw was compelling enough to make me leave (or come) at once.

When I came, I slipped in between the two: between him and my reflection, or him and his image. It was not an assertion or an insertion. Unlike a man saying: 'Am I in yet?' or 'See what a Jewish cock can do?' I was open to all comers. My coming did not end the suspense. Men asked: 'Did sex come before everything else in the world?' or 'Don't you realise there are two sides to a couple?'

I whispered in response: 'I come as if nothing has ever happened. Do you invent everything? That you see? That I am? My body is only the pretext. Some say love is impossible; or love makes everything else impossible. Others say that love is a bird or love is war or love is peace or love is a strategy with advances, expediencies, retreats, artifices, crisis techniques, based on the exception rather than the rule. Some say love is what keeps us from degenerating into norms. And others say love is the search for the perfect mirror. We can't know if it is love that unites us or if love separates us. We can never satisfy our love, our desire to be transparent; for love secretes a thick fog independently from the lovers, that shrouds everything. Love likes to pose riddles that cannot be solved, to inhabit worlds that cannot be mapped. So when choosing a mirror, remember that the mirror will outlast your presence. The mirror cannot see you.'

I, for one (or two), never knew where I was. I lived in glass. I could not be distinguished from the screen. I was not transfixed. I hovered beyond. I was constantly seen. But because I had always been secretive, and because no one had ever discovered me, I thought it sufficed to cross into the rippling glass and pretend to disappear.

Today, I broke the mirror. I didn't know I could.

Virago New Writing for the 90s

COWBOYS ARE MY WEAKNESS

Pam Houston

'Pam Houston has verve and perfect pitch . . . she snaps along in a sassy canter, her prose sharp and clean'
– *New York Times Book Review*

Sharp, touching and often hilarious, this stinging-fresh collection of short stories, from a powerful new voice, will open up new worlds of high deserts, and Alaskan tundra, of perilous white water and frozen rockies. Pam Houston's women – part daredevil, part philosopher – know they should know better, but they don't: they wrestle within themselves, with danger, and above all, with their men (whose bodies speak volumes but whose emotions are not so communicative). Sexy, gutsy and intoxicating these twelve tantalising tales are written in spare, exhilarating prose.

NOT THE END OF THE WORLD

Rebecca Stowe

'Ranks with J. D. Salinger and Carson McCullers for memorable portraits of our vulnerable young'
– Jane Rule

Twelve–year–old Maggie Pittsfield must be the luckiest girl in the world. She lives in a house with its own beach and her father owns the local candy factory. But are the Pittsfields really the perfect American family? What lies behind the mysterious and traumatic incident involving Maggie and her teacher Mr Howard? And what is Maggie evading when she escapes to the woods where the prospect of an encounter with the elusive Pervert seems much less frightening than the revelation that waits for her at home?

THEREAFTER JOHNNIE

Carolivia Herron

'Belongs in the distinguished company of Alice Walker's *The Color Purple* and Toni Morrison's *Beloved*'
– *New York Times*

Thereafter Johnnie is a bold and brilliant novel which tells of the fall of a family, the discovery of incest, and the birth of a child. Johnnie is the daughter of an incestuous union between her mother and her grandfather. More boldly still, it turns their tormented union into a strand within a larger tapestry of abuse whose origins are as old as slavery, and whose consequences are nothing less than apocalyptic. Johnnie's is a story passed down through generations, 'a swirling and terrifying epic . . . stunning and incandescent . . . luminous and visionary' (*Los Angeles Times Book Review*).

THE LAST ROOM

Elean Thomas

'Memorable . . . Thomas' Jamaican speech both sings and stings' – *Observer*

What happens when Valerie 'Putus' Barton is solemnly charged by her mother, Miss Belle, with the task of being the Barton who must take the family forward from the 'last room' of slavery into the 'mansions of the world'? Born into the third generation of African-Jamaicans after the abolition of European slavery, Putus is thus entrusted with a life mission. And so she begins a series of migrations, from the parish of St Catherine in Jamaica to a decrepit rooming-house in Birmingham; from her family, her country and ultimately from herself.

Elean Thomas has written a first novel of extraordinary perception, replete with the colour, vibrancy and rhythms of Jamaica.

WINNER OF THE 1991 RUTH HADDEN MEMORIAL PRIZE

QUEENDOM COME

Ellen Galford

**'Funny, often ingenious, fresh and strangely plausible'
– Maureen Lipman**

Something is fishy in the state of Scotland when a businessman is stabbed where it hurts during a druidical meeting on Arthur's seat. During the 'reign' of a rather dominating female Prime Minister, the Ancient Briton and magnificent virago, Albanna, has returned to her Queendom, demanding an excess of regal attention and Chinese takeaways. With the help of her lesbian High Priestess Gwhyldis, she is fulfilling a promise made to deliver her people in times of trouble . . .

In *Queendom Come*, Ellen Galford combines the contemporary gusto of Jeanette Winterson with the high satire of Swift and Pope – adding an irresistible humour and vision which is all her own.

Virago also publish *Moll Cutpurse: Her True History, The Dyke and the Dybbuk* is forthcoming, 1993.

WINTER HUNGER

Ann Tracy

This chilling novel tells an enigmatic and haunting story, set in the frozen wilderness of Northern Manitoba. Fleeing Toronto with his obsessively loved wife Diana and their infant son Cam, Alan Hooper, a would-be anthropologist, ventures out to a Chipewayan Reserve on Wino Day Lake to study the kinship and food-gathering patterns of three native communities. As the darkness of winter overcomes the light Alan discovers a savage landscape which abhors a human presence, an alien culture which tolerates the ever-present possibility of death and the phantom spirit of the dreaded Windigo. While Alan endeavours to save himself from impending madness, Diana, now firmly ensconced in their new life, inexplicably withdraws . . . Ann Tracy's Gothic tale, written in crisp, sardonic prose, at once emphasises and subverts the increasing horror at the heart of this frozen wilderness.